VALLEY OF HUNTED MEN

Valley of
Hunted Men

Bradford Scott

**WHEELER
CHIVERS**

This Large Print edition is published by Wheeler Publishing, Waterville, Maine USA and by BBC Audiobooks Ltd, Bath, England.

Wheeler Publishing is an imprint of Thomson Gale, a part of The Thomson Corporation.

Wheeler is a trademark and used herein under license.

The text of this Large Print edition is unabridged.

Other aspects of the book may vary from the original edition.

Set in 16 pt. Plantin.

LIBRARY OF CONGRESS CATALOGING-IN-PUBLICATION DATA

Scott, Bradford, 1893–1975.
  Valley of hunted men / by Bradford Scott.
    p. cm. — (Wheeler Publishing large print western)
    ISBN-13: 978-1-59722-448-2 (softcover : alk. paper)
    ISBN-10: 1-59722-448-0 (softcover : alk. paper) 1. Texas — Fiction. 2. Large
type books. I. Title.
PS3537.C9265V36 2007
813'.52—dc22   2006035238

BRITISH LIBRARY CATALOGUING-IN-PUBLICATION DATA AVAILABLE

Published in 2007 in the U.S. by arrangement with
Golden West Literary Agency.
Published in 2007 in the U.K. by arrangement with Golden West Literary Agency.

U.K. Hardcover: 978 1 405 64026 8 (Chivers Large Print)
U.K. Softcover: 978 1 405 64027 5 (Camden Large Print)

Printed in the United States of America on permanent paper
10 9 8 7 6 5 4 3 2 1

VALLEY OF HUNTED MEN

ONE

An almost pathless jungle, the Big Thicket rolls north and east for a hundred miles and more, in places better than forty miles in width. Two million acres of mystery and death! The rustling leaves of towering pine and oak whisper of bloody deeds done in the eternal twilight beneath their interlacing branches. This is the dark empire of hunted men, of the lawless and the damned. Here slithers old Coffin Head, the giant rattle-snake, "big around as a man's leg and fourteen feet long." Here, when the Gulf winds roar through the tree tops, witches and warlocks and "little men in green" ride the wings of the storm and hold high revel under the orbed moon. The Big Thicket is neither swamp or marshland, but dry and rich soil. But in its depths are strange glassy pools, reed-fringed, where the alligator "sings" and every variety of waterfowl cluster; and widening bayous sometimes form small muskegs. There is also Lost Creek, which drops suddenly into a hole between Bragg and Honey Islands, to re-appear just as suddenly from under a bank of ferns more than five miles to the south.

To Ranger Walt Slade, the arboreal marvel rising from the rangeland had the mien of a vast, crouching, prehistoric beast waiting to engulf its prey. It seemed strange that only a dozen miles south of this scene of primeval solitude was the roaring oil-boom town of Beaumont, as wild as any gold camp of the Old West, where fortunes were made and lost in a day and the spindletop gushers were due to change the economic life of America.

Sitting Shadow, his great black horse, the man the *peons* of the Rio Grande river vil-lages named *El Halcon* — The Hawk — the last rays of the setting sun etching his sternly handsome profile in flame, lent an interesting and striking touch of life to the lonely landscape. Very tall, more than six feet, the width of his shoulders and the depth of his chest matched his height. His deeply bronzed face was dominated by long, black-lashed eyes of pale gray — gay, reck-less eyes that despite their coldness seemed to have little devils of laughter in their depths. At times, however, those "devils" would leap to the fore and were *not* laughing. His rather wide mouth, grin-quirked at the corners, somewhat relieved the tinge of sternness, almost fierceness, evinced by the prominent high-bridged nose above and the lean, powerful chin and jaw beneath. His pushed-back "J.B." revealed crisp, thick hair so black a blue shadow seemed to lie upon it.

Slade wore the homely but efficient garb of the rangeland, and wore it with the careless grace with which a clubman wears evening clothes — faded Levis and blue shirt, vivid neckerchief looped about his sinewy throat, well-scuffed half-boots of softly tanned leather. Around his lean waist were double cartridge belts, and from the carefully worked and oiled cut-out holsters protruded the plan back butts of heavy guns. A Winchester rifle was snug in the saddle boot beneath his left thigh.

Hooking one long leg comfortably over the saddle horn, Slade rolled a cigarette with the slim fingers of his left hand. He smoked in leisurely fashion, surveying the gloomy and desolate terrain that was the Big Thicket.

"Shadow," he said, "it's one heck of a section, but I've a notion we're going to find ourselves mixed up in it before our chore over this way is finished."

The black horse snorted and scanned the wild tangle with disfavor.

"Yep, sort of thorny in there, the chances are," Slade chuckled. "Wouldn't be surprised if we both lose a few patches of hide if we have to sashay through — Now what!"

Thin with distance had sounded what was indubitably a rifle shot. Slade's gaze shifted from the Big Thicket to the northwest. A mile to the north and fully that distance to the west he saw a bobbing blob that was a horseman speeding east. Six or seven hundred yards to the rear were a number of bouncing dots; Slade counted eight in all. They were directly in line with the first rider who apparently was making for the Big Thicket.

Slade wondered what was going on, a sheriff's posse chasing a lawbreaker? Looked sort of that way, but he wasn't sure. Strange things had been happening in this section of late, which was the reason why Walt Slade was where he was. He leaned forward in the saddle, his eyes fixed on the race with death as the forfeit if the leading horseman lost. Now Slade could see that the quarry rode a tall roan horse that had speed.

But the mounts of the pursuers also had speed, a little more than the roan could boast; they were closing the distance. Smoke puffed from their ranks and to Slade drifted the brittle crackle of the reports. Again they fired, and again. The fusillade continued. Tense, eager, the ranger watched; there was nothing he could do about it, even if he knew what the dickens to do. Hardly the sort of thing for a lone rider to horn into, especially as he had no way of knowing who was right and who was wrong. His sympathy was with the speeding horseman, although he knew it could well be misplaced sympathy.

"Another quarter of a mile and he'll hit the brush and should be safe," he told Shadow. "Maybe he'll make it."

The rider didn't. The quarter of a mile shrank to less than four hundred yards, to three. Abruptly the pursuers jerked to a halt. Rifles took deliberate aim, spurted smoke. The speeding horseman spun from the saddle to lie writhing on the ground. His mount cantered on a few yards, paused and gazed back. The pursuers sent their horses charging forward. They reached the writhing body, but did not draw rein. The foremost, who appeared tall and broad-shouldered, leaned over and deliberately fired three shots with a six-gun. The body jerked and was still. The group rode on without slackening speed. Another moment and the dark shadow of the Big Thicket swallowed them.

Slade relaxed in the saddle, exhaling the breath he had unconsciously been holding.

"Shadow," he said, his usually musical voice hard and brittle, "Shadow, that was no sheriff's posse. What we saw was a deliberate and cold-blooded killing. This will stand a mite of investigating. Wonder if those hellions spotted us down here?"

He glanced at the sun. Only a narrow curve of its red cricle showed above the horizon; it quickly dimmed from sight and shadows began creeping over the rangeland; the Big Thicket was already a solid block of gloom.

"We'll wait a few minutes and then we'll mosey up there for a look at that poor devil," he told the horse. "Might be a good idea, though, to try and give those gents a sort of wrong slant if they happened to stop to keep an eye on us. Let's go, feller!"

With which he turned Shadow's head west and cantered across the range at a good pace, slanting a glance now and then at the sinister gloom of the sprawling growth looming black and ominous against the darkening sky. He shook his head as he glanced at the almost full moon rising in the east. That moon would cast more light than he cared for at the moment. Well, there was no help for it, and for the time being the shadow of the Thicket would extend for some distance across the prairie.

Slade rode for a mile and more before he veered to the north. Another mile and he turned due east in line with where the body of the slain man lay, slowing Shadow's pace, his eyes never leaving the tangle of growth that drew steadily nearer.

However, there was no sign of movement in the outer fringe of the chaparral. No sound broke the great stillness save the calls of night birds and the yipping of a distant coyote talking to the moon. He reached the body, swung from the saddle, sliding his Winchester from the boot, his eyes still on the edge of the thicket.

From the black shadows spurted fire; and before the echoes could slam back from the trees, the tall form of *El Halcon* pitched forward to lie as motionless as the body of the dead man back of which it fell.

Two

As he fell, Slade thrust the rifle barrel across the corpse, its black muzzle trained on the growth. Just in time he had seen movement amid the shadows. Now he lay with the butt of the long gun clamped to his shoulder, his icy eyes glancing along the sights.

For minutes he lay thus, scarcely breathing, waiting. He had heard no sound of retreating hoofbeats after the shot was fired, neither of a single horse nor a troop. Somebody was still there, watching, listening.

Again the ripple of a shadow amid the shadows. The Winchester gushed orange flame, the report like a thunderclap in the silence. With a bubbling scream, a man fairly leaped from the sheltering growth to come down with limbs all a-sprawl. The rifle boomed a drumroll as Slade fired as fast as he could work the ejection lever, spraying the brush back and forth with lead until the magazine was empty. He heard a yelp of pain, a torrent of oaths, then a thudding of hoofs quickly dying into the depths of the Thicket. He reloaded the Winchester and lay peering and listening.

Had the killers kept on going, all of them? There was no sound of returning hoofbeats, but one might have lingered, and the others might have dismounted to steal back on foot. He flipped his hat onto the rifle muzzle and thrust it into the air to simulate the movement of a man getting swiftly to his feet.

Nothing happened; the silence remained unbroken. The moon was now slanting light across the outer fringe of the growth, and Slade decided to take a chance. Leaping to his feet, he ducked and weaved to where the dead man's well-trained horse still stood. Still nothing happened. He talked soothingly to the horse as he drew near. The animal pricked its ears and blew softly through its nose and made no attempt to move off. Slade gripped the bit iron and led it to where the dead man lay. Without effort he lifted the heavy form and draped it across the saddle, securing it in place with a "piggin' string," or tie rope, that was looped ready to hand; evidently the dead man was a cowboy. A shaft of moonlight revealed a bronzed, big-featured face and grizzled hair, which was all Slade had time to note at the moment. He yearned for a look at the dead killer who lay at the edge of the growth; but it would be foolhardy to approach the thicket. There was a chance that the fellow's companions, once they got over their scare, might come stealing back on foot to exact vengeance on his killer. Mounting Shadow and looping the reins of the burdened horse about his wrist, he rode south at a fast pace, glancing over his shoulder from time to time.

However, he saw no signs of pursuit and now the moonlight made the prairie almost as bright as day. South by east he rode, toward where Beaumont boomed and thundered under the stars. The oil town was the county seat of Jefferson County and the sheriff would have an office there.

Slade knew that Beaumont was a going concern long before Tony Lucas, drilling for oil out on the prairie south of the town, brought in the gusher that heralded the opening of the great Spindletop field. First, lumbering was Beaumont's foremost activity. Shingles were made by sawing logs into shingle lengths, splitting these cuts into proper thickness and thinning the edges with a drawing knife. Then cotton, sugar cane and cattle were produced by southern planters who settled in the vicinity. There was a sixty foot depth in the Neches River at the end of Main Street, and nosing through Sabine Pass and up the Neches, Gulf schooners and side-wheel river boats carried on a busy traffic in cotton, cattle, and shingles, thus early laying the foundation of the town's importance as a port.

Next, gentlemen who saw opportunity in the rich lowlands began to plant rice. They ran fences and the cattlemen of the section, who had little liking for barbed wire, objected with six-shooters. The rice planters explained their position with others of similar calibre and things were quite merry until the rival factions finally decided it was possible to grow rice and raise cows amicably without the help of powdersmoke. Lumber, rice and cattle all tended to bring prosperity and riotous living. Beaumont was not tame.

Then came the oil strike, and Beaumont really reared up on its hind legs and howled.

Beaumont. "Beautiful Hill!" The hill was still there the night Walt Slade rode into the oil town, but there was little of beauty!

Beaumont never slept and was going strong as Slade headed for the courthouse between Main and Pearl Streets, with the led horse bearing its grisly burden. He received stares a-plenty but nobody questioned him. Even this unusual sight could not shake Beaumont's aplomb.

Late as it was, a light burned in the sheriff's office; Beaumont peace officers didn't sleep much. The sheriff, a grizzled oldtimer of the rangeland, looked up inquiringly from his desk as Slade entered.

"Something I can do for you, son?" he asked.

"Yes," Slade replied, "you can come outside and take a look at what I brought in; you'll want to take charge of it."

The puzzled law officer followed Slade out the door. He uttered an exclamation as his eyes fell on what the led horse bore.

"Where in blazes did you get that?" he demanded.

"Up by the Big Thicket," Slade replied. "There's another one up there by the edge of the growth you may want to pack in; I could handle only one."

The sheriff profanely expressed his bewilderment. "Guess you'll have to do some explaining before I can get head or tail of this loco business," he said. "First, though, I'll take a look at this one. Untie him and we'll pack him into the office."

Slade undid the tie rope and lifted the body from the saddle. For the first time the

18

sheriff got a look at the dead man's face. He started back.

"Good God!" he exclaimed. "It's Cliff Tevis, Dunlap Jefferson's range boss!" He whirled to face Slade, his eyes filled with suspicion. "Guess you will have to do some explaining, and fast," he said harshly. "All right, bring him in, bring him in and lay him on the floor."

Slade did so, folding the dead hands on the breast. The sheriff fetched a blanket with which the corpse was covered. He gestured to a chair. Slade sat down and rolled a cigarette.

"Now," said the sheriff, "let's have it. How did Cliff Tevis get cashed in?"

Slade told him, in detail. Gradually the suspicion faded from the sheriff's frosty eyes.

"Reckon you're telling a straight story, or you'd hardly have packed him in here," he said. His face darkened with wrath.

"And they gunned poor Cliff while he was layin' on the ground kicking!"

Slade nodded.

"And you say you got one of the hellions?"

"Yes, after he nearly got me," Slade replied. "I felt the wind of that blue whistler he threw at me."

"I hope you got the one you heard yelp

through the belly, and left him to die sweatin'," the sheriff said vindictively. "I sure hope so! A pity you didn't get a look at the one you downed. But as you said, it would have been a darn fool thing to do, ride up to that patch of devil's brush. Poor old Cliff; he was a good feller. Everybody liked him, even the oil people, though he was Dunlap Jefferson's righthand man."

"What's wrong with Jefferson?" Slade asked casually.

"Oh, nothing, except he's kinda uppity," the sheriff replied. "The Jefferson family has always had a lot to say as to what was done in this section, but that's sorta changing since the oil strike. Jeff has no use for the oil folks and fights them tooth and nail. He says the strike has brought in lawless riff-raff that's making trouble for everybody. He ain't far wrong, there. Says the whole section is being ruined, that the oil fumes kill cows and poison the waterholes."

"That's in the nature of superstition," Slade said.

"Maybe, but you'd have trouble making Jefferson believe it," said the sheriff. "That goes for a lot of the other cowmen, too. Also the strike has brought in a flock of wildcatters — independent oil men, with a drilling rig and hopes. They're nosing around everywhere, thinking maybe they'll open up another Spindletop. Jefferson found an outfit drilling on land he claims over to the west of here, and chased 'em away. Did the same for another bunch. A week later, he had a barn burned."

Slade nodded thoughtfully. "You said, I believe, that they were drilling on land Jefferson claims?" he remarked.

"Uh-huh, but I guess it's really open range. You know, the big fellers sometimes claim a lot of land they ain't got title to."

"And which is really state land," Slade said.

"That's right, I reckon," conceded the sheriff, "but they claim by right of occupancy over a long period of time. Jefferson owns the Diamond ranch, the biggest and best in the section; he has plenty of land, and, as I said, claims a lot more. He's always got away with it — has influence down at the capital, but there are some big men interested in the oil development here and hard to buck, even for Dunlap Jefferson. Fellers like ex-governor Jim Hogg, and Bet-a-Million Gates, and Jim Swayne, and J. S. Cullinan, to name a few. Jefferson's set and willing to take 'em all on, though. He says money ain't everything, that the business end of a six-shooter talks louder than a dollar. Got something there."

"He has," Slade smiled, "but promiscuous use of a six-shooter sometimes means trouble for everybody, including the innocent bystander," he added.

"Guess that's right," agreed the sheriff. "Anyhow, it don't make a peace officer's chore any easier. Jefferson is going to be fit to be hogtied when he hears about Cliff, and he'll blame the oil folks for it, sure as shooting."

"The men who killed Tevis rode like rangehands," Slade observed thoughtfully. "I doubt if many oil workers could back a horse that way."

"Jefferson will say they hired some sidewinders to do the chore — plenty of that sort hanging around here now," said the sheriff.

"Something to think about," Slade acceded. "Well, I'm going to get me a square meal and then locate a place to sleep."

"Plenty of hotels in Beaumont," the sheriff said. "The Crosby House is about at the top, only the tariff is a mite higher than at the places the cowboys usually pound their ears in, like the Humboldt over on Austin Street. Everybody hangs out in the Crosby House lobby and at the bar at one time or another, though. Big oil men, drillers, cowhands, and others."

"Guess the Crosby House will do," Slade replied.

"Corner of Orleans and Crockett Streets," directed the sheriff. "Anybody will show you the way. You'll be around tomorrow, of course? We'll want to hold an inquest on poor Cliff."

"I will," Slade said.

Later, while rehashing the incident and the conversation with his chief deputy, the sheriff remarked, "When he said that, the big hellion gave me a sort of funny feeling. All of a sudden his voice changed. Mighty nice talking voice before. Got a notion the feller can sing. But when he said that, it was sorta like a steel tire grinding on ice. And his eyes changed, too. Seemed to get paler and look way off. I sure wouldn't want to have him look that way at me and mean it. Another funny thing. Circumstances being what they were, I was all primed to learn everything I could about him, but after he'd left, it all of a sudden came to me that I'd been spilling my guts and he hadn't said a darn thing. I didn't know any more about him than I did when he walked in the door!"

Other and smarter men than Sheriff Tom Colton had registered a similar complaint of Walt Slade's uncanny ability to inveigle the other fellow into doing all the talking.

At the door, Slade paused. "Sheriff," he said, "don't you think it would be a good notion for you and me to ride to the Big Thicket tomorrow and bring in that body? Give you a chance to hold a double-barreled inquest."

"Why, I guess it would be," the sheriff admitted. "I'll meet you here at the office at ten in the morning. Okay?"

"Okay," Slade agreed.

"By the way, I'll look after Cliff's horse," the sheriff called. "Leave it at the rack."

Slade had visited Beaumont prior to the oil strike and knew his way around. He found quarters for his horse not far from the sheriff's office, enjoyed a good meal in an all-night restaurant and repaired to the Crosby House where he registered for a room, in which he deposited his saddle pouches and rifle. Not feeling particularly sleepy, he descended to the big lobby, sat down and rolled a cigarette, surveying with interest the busy and colorful scene.

Although it was well past midnight, the Crosby House was still going strong. Slade could see that the long bar was crowded, likewise the dining room. Most of the chairs in the lobby were occupied, often drawn together in clusters by men who talked in

24

low tones with their heads close together.

Slade knew that the Crosby House was the "pit," the "curb," and "exchange" of the oil industry and that millions of dollars changed hands in its lobby and rooms, and the lobby was the lounging place of men with their ears open to opportunity of one sort or another. He was studying the gathering when he noticed a big distinguished-looking man making his way across the room. Slade recognized James S. Hogg, former governor of Texas, now one of Beaumont's oil titans.

Hogg, glancing about the room, suddenly halted in his stride. Then he hurried forward, hand outstretched.

"Slade!" he exclaimed. "What the devil are *you* doing here?"

"Dropped in to see the sights," Slade smiled as they shook hands warmly.

"Like the devil!" chuckled the ex-governor as he drew up a chair. "A likely story! You're here on business, that I'll wager. I smell gunpowder! How's McNelty?"

"Fine as frog hair," Slade replied. "He'll be pleased to know I met you."

"Give him my regards," said Hogg. "Never was a finer man than old Jim. I'm glad you're here, Slade, we've been having considerable trouble in this section of late,

25

and I mean bad trouble."

"I can believe that," Slade observed. "I got a nice reception."

Hogg glanced at him inquiringly and Slade regaled him with an account of what happened at the edge of the Big Thicket. The former governor shook his head.

"Getting worse all the time," he commented. "The Twilight Riders again, I'll bet my last peso."

"The Twilight Riders?"

"That's what somebody named them, claiming they're lineal and fit descendants of the hellions who used to operate in the no-man's land east of the Sabine in Louisiana. Both the United States and Mexico claimed the land and the region was a kind of twilight zone with nobody knowing for sure who exercised lawful authority over it, with the result that there was a minimum of recognized authority of any kind. Colonists were pushing through the section and became the prey for that gang of robbers, murderers and rapists called the Twilighters. The bunch operating in this section have quite a few traits in common with that outfit, so that's how the name, the Twilight Riders, got hung onto them. Guess it fits. Also it seems that the hours just before and after dusk are their favorite time for pulling their hellishness. At first, their only purpose appeared to be to harass the oil field. An outlying well was set on fire and if the wind hadn't shifted about that time, there was a chance that the whole field would have gone up in smoke. Then a couple of derricks were dynamited. Oil workers were beaten, going to and from work or in the Beaumont saloons; freight wagons packing supplies were overturned, the horses shot, the drivers mauled."

Hogg paused to light a cigar. Slade rolled another cigarette and waited expectantly.

"All that was bad enough," Hogg resumed, "but there was worse to come. We've had payroll robberies, with the guards killed. A bank robbery. Altogether, a devil of a situation. One to tax even *El Halcon's* courage and ingenuity, I'm afraid."

"Possibly," Slade conceded. "Thanks for the compliments. If I happen to have any of either, the chances are I'll need all I've got."

"I have every confidence in your ability to handle the situation," Hogg declared, adding, "and so has McNelty. Otherwise he'd hardly have sent you here alone."

"Oh, Captain Jim gets tired of my hanging around, after a while, and will do anything to get rid of me for a bit," Slade smiled. "By the way, it looks as if there is some smart and capable individual heading that bunch. Got any suspects?"

The ex-governor hesitated a moment before replying. "There is a man in this section who is bitterly inimical to the oil field," he said slowly. "A big ranch owner, the biggest in the section, I guess. I've a notion he would do most anything to make trouble for the field, which he insists encroaches on his holdings and is detrimental to his interest and violates the lawful rights of property. His name is Dunlap Jefferson, a descendant of about the oldest cattle-raising family hereabouts. As I said, he'd do almost anything to harass the oil operators, but I can hardly see him heading a gang of robbers and murderers."

"Not wittingly, perhaps," Slade said, "but when a man starts dealing with the kind of people he needs for such things as blowing up derricks and setting fire to oil wells, he's letting himself in for almost anything. You'll recall, sir, what happened in Lincoln County, New Mexico. John Chisum and Major Murphy hired tough gunfighters to do their fighting in the row that had developed between them, including such characters as Billy the Kid, Bill Morton, Frank McNab, Doc Skurlock, and Charley Bowdre, among others. Frontier ruffians of the worst sort. Very quickly they got out of hand. The result — robberies, cattle stealing and killings, some of them cold-blooded murders. Both Chisum and Murphy disavowed responsibility. They had, of course, not intended such happenings and were appalled by them; but the fact remains that they had been responsible for the influx of desperadoes. Just such a thing could have happened to this man, Jefferson. That is if he is really mixed up in the business. I gather there is nothing definite against him."

"Nothing," admitted Hogg, "but a lot of people are darn suspicious."

"Suspicion isn't proof," Slade smiled, "so I guess I'll have to hold my judgment in abeyance, for the time being, at least."

The ex-governor nodded and stood up. "I'll have to be going," he said. "Drop around tomorrow evening if you can. I'd like for you to meet some of the boys. Gates, and Swayne and Cullinan, and some others. You'll like them. You ought to come in with us here, Walt. With your education and brains and ability, you could make a fortune in no time."

"Perhaps," conceded Slade, with another smile. "But I rather like my work and I get considerable satisfaction in thinking that now and then it makes the going a mite easier for worthwhile folks. More than I'd get out of a lot of money, I imagine."

Jim Hogg gazed at him a moment. There was a touch of admiration in that look, perhaps; the unconscious tribute of the man whose life has been spent in the conquest of material things to the man who has the audacity, insensate though it seem, to fling these to the winds in his search after ideals. Jim Hogg was a good man, and he was on his way to become a very rich man, but he sighed slightly as he turned to the crowded lobby where the "golden calf" was held aloft for men to worship.

THREE

Slade sat smoking for a while longer. Jim Hogg's remarks had brought on a retrospective mood and he was thinking of the past.

Shortly after Walt Slade graduated from a famous college of engineering, his father had suffered business reverses which entailed the loss of his ranch. Soon afterward, he died. Walt had intended to take a postgraduate course to round out his education. This, however, became impossible for the time being and when Captain Jim McNelty, commander of the famous "Frontier Battalion" of the Texas Rangers, suggested that he come into the rangers for a while and pursue his studies in spare time, Slade, who had worked some with Captain Jim during summer vacations, thought the notion a good one. Long since, he had gotten everything and more from private study than he could have hoped to have acquired from the postgrad course; he was all set to enter the profession which he had intended to be his life work.

But meanwhile, ranger work had gotten a strong hold on him and he was loath to sever connections with the illustrious body of law enforcement officers. He was young and there was plenty of time to be an engineer; he'd stick with the rangers for a while.

Due to his habit of working undercover whenever possible and often not revealing his ranger connections, Walt Slade had over the course of the years built up a peculiar dual reputation. To those who knew the truth, Captain McNelty's lieutenant and ace-man was looked upon as the ablest and most fearless ranger of them all. Others who did *not* know the truth, including some puzzled sheriffs and marshals, were wont to declare that *El Halcon* was just a blasted outlaw too smart to get caught.

Slade did nothing to counteract this erroneous state of affairs, although, as Captain Jim had more than once pointed out, it laid him open to grave personal danger.

"Some trigger-happy sheriff or deputy will plug you sometime," Captain Jim would growl. "Or some darn owlhoot or quick-draw man out to get a reputation by downing the notorious *El Halcon* might gun you."

"Possibly," Slade would concede, "but it opens up avenues of information that would be closed to a known peace officer. Of course, sir, if you forbid —"

"Oh, go ahead, blast you!" Captain Jim would interrupt. "After all, it's your funeral, and that's just what it's liable to end up — your *funeral!*"

So Walt Slade went on his carefree way and attended quite a few funerals, but not as the principal attraction.

Slade wondered why the sheriff had not seen fit to mention the Twilight Riders in the course of their conversation. However, there could well be one or two plausible explanations why he refrained from doing so. Slade had gathered from Jim Hogg's remarks that folks who talked too freely about the Riders, by remarkable "coincidence," sooner or later came to grief in one way or another, usually sooner. Which may have accounted for the sheriff's reluctance to discuss them with a stranger. Also, it was not improbable that the peace officer was indebted to Dunlap Jefferson for past favors. A man of Jefferson's calibre would undoubtedly be able to swing quite a few votes in the section, and Sheriff Colton had been elected to office prior to the oil strike and the resulting influx of new citizens who might hold more independent views. Which, if so, considering the rumors anent Dunlap Jefferson's possible connection with the Twilight Riders, put the sheriff on something of a spot. Slade pinched out his cigarette and went to bed.

Slade and the sheriff, leading a spare horse, left Beaumont shortly after ten the following morning. They rode steadily at a good pace and without incident reached the edge of the Big Thicket. With the plainsman's sense of distance and direction, Slade quickly located the spot where the body of the slain outlaw lay.

The dead man proved to be an unsavory looking specimen with no particularly outstanding features. He was short and squat with a broad face, the nostrils fleshy at the base, the mouth a thin line across his swarthy countenance, and very dark eyes and hair.

"Looks like he might have some Injun blood," commented the sheriff as he began turning out the contents of the fellow's pockets.

"Nothing that means anything, aside from more money than his sort had any business having," he grunted. "We'll tie him on the spare horse and pack him to town. Maybe somebody there can remember something about him. See you got him through the neck."

Slade nodded, the concentration furrow deep between his black brows, a sign that *El Halcon* was doing some thinking. For Slade noticed something the sheriff overlooked; the seams of the dead man's overall pockets were caked with oily dust, an indication that he spent more than a little time around the oil field. There were no callouses made by wrench, spanner or crowbar on his stubby hands; of course, though, there were plenty of chores around the field other than manual labor.

But the fellow's garb, from high-heeled spurred boots to broad-brimmed Stetson secured by a chin strap, was that of a range rider, and his hands did show marks of rope and branding iron, not new but plain enough. Also, on the ornate brass buckle of his gun belt, rubbed almost smooth, and undecipherable, was what had undoubtedly been a brand mark.

His rifle lay nearby, a good iron. Slade noted that the front sight had been filed thin, the notch of the rear sight very narrow. Quite likely the fellow had been the marksman of the band, detailed to slink forward on foot to undertake the chore of murder that had cost him his life.

All of which the ranger found very interesting, and which he refrained from discussing with the sheriff.

The sheriff was turning toward the spare horse, preparatory to placing it alongside the body when Slade spoke.

"This fellow had a horse," he said. "Maybe we can locate it, if it didn't follow the others. Suppose we nose around in the brush a little on the chance it's still hanging around."

"By gosh, that's a notion," replied Colton. "I didn't think of it. Let's go."

They entered the growth, which was dense at the edge of the forest but quickly thinned. Sheriff Colton peered around bushes and into thickets, muttering to himself. Slade, on the other hand, was silent and kept his eyes fixed on the ground.

"Here's where they waited for that jigger to slide up to the edge of the brush and do his chore," he suddenly announced. He gestured to the ground as he spoke, which was not particularly soft.

Sheriff Colton peered close and was finally able to make out the prints left by a number of horses.

"Looks like you're right," he agreed dubiously. "Don't think I'd have spotted them; those eyes of yours must be sort of out of the ordinary."

"Here, they go away, in a hurry," Slade added a moment later. "Guess my blue whistlers came sort of close. Appears they headed for the depths of the Thicket. Now let's see about the horse that fellow rode. No, I don't think it followed the others. Only seven sets of prints, as far as I can make out, and there were eight riders in the bunch that killed Tevis."

The sheriff shook his head in wordless admiration and waited expectantly as Slade quartered the ground in the vicinity of the clump of iron marks made by stationary horses.

"Here it is," Slade said. "One horse diagonaling into the growth; hunting grass, the chances are. Come along, they're easy to follow."

"Son, you sure you ain't part Injun?" asked the sheriff. "Never knew a full white man able to follow tracks on hard ground like you do."

"Could be," Slade replied cheerfully. "Hard to tell what you'll find in your ancestry, if you go back far enough. Never heard about it, but it could be so. Funny fruit sometimes hangs on a family tree."

"Wouldn't care to have too many limbs climbed in mine," chuckled the sheriff. "Seems I rec'lect my grandmother having a twinkle in her eye."

Slade's keen eyes had no trouble following the tracks left by the wandering horse. Only a few hundred yards farther on, they found the animal in a grassy glade, a saddle twisted sideways on its back, trying to graze but having difficulty because of the bit in its mouth. Slade approached the cayuse, talking to it in soothing tones. The horse made no attempt to run away but looked grateful as he flipped the bit from its mouth and removed the saddle.

Meanwhile, Sheriff Colton was standing stock still, staring at the beast's haunch, on which was burned a clean-cut *Diamond*.

Slade said nothing, but there was a hint of amusement in his eyes as he gazed at the sheriff, whose mouth was hanging open slightly, a dazed expression on his face.

"Recognize the burn?" Slade asked casually.

The sheriff shot him an exasperated glance. "You know darn well I do," he growled. "Well, if this don't take the shingles off the barn!"

"Not necessarily," Slade pointed out.

"Don't go looking sideways at your *amigo* Jefferson until you know for sure *why* you are looking. Horses can be bought, or stolen."

"That's right," the sheriff conceded slowly, "but it looks darn funny."

"Would seem a bit funnier, misusing the word, wouldn't it, to think that a man working for Jefferson would take part in the murder of Jefferson's range boss? That is, unless it happened to be a grudge killing, and it seems hardly likely that all eight of that bunch had a grudge against Cliff Tevis, whom you said was well-liked and had no enemies."

"Guess that's right, too," replied the sheriff. "But what in blazes does it mean?"

"Hard to tell," Slade replied evasively. "Unless there happened to be something in Tevis' life that was not generally known."

"Don't know what the devil it could be," said the sheriff. "As I said, everybody seemed to like Cliff, even Jefferson, who's not much on liking anybody. He thought mighty well of Cliff, even though they didn't always agree on things. Argued to beat heck at times. I happen to know Cliff didn't favor Jeff's row with the oil people and told him so. Told him he was bucking a stacked deck, that he couldn't stop progress and there was no sense in trying to. Said the sensible thing was to get along with them, sell them all the beef cows they needed and take a nice profit from them instead of standing on his hind legs and pawing sand. Didn't set too well with old Jeff, but I've a notion it gave him something to think about. He always found out that any advice Cliff gave him was to his own advantage, even though he was sometimes too bullheaded to listen. I'm afraid this was one of the times."

Slade had let the sheriff ramble on, for he found the information relative to the relationship of Dunlap Jefferson and his range boss interesting. Abruptly, however, he ceased to listen to what Colton was saying. Without warning his long arm shot out and slammed the sheriff off his feet. He himself hit the ground at almost the same instant.

A bullet screamed through the air over their prostrate forms. Another kicked dirt in Slade's face. He drew and shot from the hip, again and again. An agonized shriek echoed the second report, a wailing curse the third, then a crashing of the brush on the far side of the glade. *El Halcon* bounded erect and leaped in the direction of the sound; but at that instant the swearing sheriff reared up on hands and knees and

Slade took a header over him. Colton flattened out with a strangled squawk. Slade again got to his feet, a trifle shakily, for the fall had been a hard one. To his ears came the beat of fast hoofs pounding off through the growth. He relaxed, his eyes never leaving the screen of brush across the glade, from which came a queer gabbling sound and a thrashing about.

"Steady," he told the sheriff, over his shoulder. "I think I downed one of them, but he isn't dead and one of that sort, wounded, is dangerous as a broken-back rattler. Circle around to the left a little and we'll see what we can find out; try not to make a noise."

The sheriff ceased swearing and followed Slade across the clearing. Once inside the screen of brush, Slade moved slowly and with care. A moment later he paused, staring ahead.

"Come along," he told the sheriff. "He's harmless."

The wounded drygulcher, blood still pulsing from severed arteries, was going fast. The heavy slug from Slade's Colt had torn off one side of his lower jaw. As Slade bent over him, his exposed tongue wagged as if he were trying to say something, but only a thin gibber came from his throat. His chest arched mightily as he fought for air, fell in, and did not rise again.

"Pity he didn't last long enough to talk a little," Slade observed. "Might have handed out some valuable information."

"Guess he couldn't have said anything anybody could understand," mumbled the sheriff who, although a hardened oldtimer, was a little white. "Blazes, what a horrible looking mess!"

Slade nodded. "I think I nicked the other one, from the way he yelped," he observed. "Not enough to stop him, though. No use to try and follow him, he's got a head start. And we might run into some more of the bunch unexpectedly. We're lucky as it is."

"How did you catch on?" asked the sheriff.

"Heard a little crackling in the brush and saw movement there," Slade replied. "Figured it was best for us to hit the dirt; guess it was."

"Son," the sheriff said, "I figure you saved my life by slapping me to the ground, and chanced losing your own by taking time to do it. I won't forget. Anytime, anyway I can lend you a hand, ask and ask quick."

"Perhaps I will sometime, never can tell," Slade replied with a smile. "Now suppose we give this specimen a once-over."

"Think some more of the hellions might come along, looking for him?" the sheriff asked apprehensively.

"I'll know it if they do," Slade answered briefly as he squatted beside the corpse.

In contrast to the first drygulcher, the fellow was lean and lanky with bristly red hair. His mangled features were so covered with blood there was no making much of them. His fixed eyes were blue.

A careful examination revealed nothing of importance. There was dust in the pocket seams, but it was not impregnated with oil.

"Now let's see about his horse," Slade suggested. "Should be tied somewhere close by."

It was, to a tree, a good looking animal. Sheriff Colton swore explosively as he viewed it, for it also bore a Diamond brand.

"Guess we might as well tie the hellion to its back and head back to town," he said.

"Sheriff," Slade differed, "I don't think that's a good idea. That brand will cause a lot of talk and is liable to make folks jump to conclusions that may be all wrong. I don't see any sense in perhaps starting a corpse-and-cartridge session between Dunlap Jefferson and his hands and some of the oil men. I believe it will be best to get the rig off the critter and turn it loose with the other one. The spare horse we brought along will pack both bodies."

The sheriff tugged his mustache thoughtfully. "I've a notion you're right," he said. "Okay, we'll do just that. Let's get going before some more of the hellions come along and stumble onto us like the other two did." He appeared struck by a sudden thought. "Or did they just stumble onto us?" he added.

"I doubt it," Slade replied. "I'd say they either figured we'd be coming up here for the body, although I think that is a bit far-fetched, or, which is more reasonable, that somebody watched us ride out of town and circled around to get here ahead of us and set the trap. Easy to guess where we were headed, with a spare horse. Yes, I've a notion that was it."

"The ornery sidewinders!" growled the sheriff. "Drygulching a peace officer!" He shot Slade a shrewd glance.

"Son, that's what you should be, a peace officer, instead of riding the chuck line, as I suppose you are. You'd make a good one."

Slade smiled, but did not comment.

FOUR

As they rode away from the Thicket, the led horse packing the two bodies, Slade kept a sharp watch on the outer fringe of the growth for a thousand yards or more, although he hardly expected further trouble. Afterward he glanced back now and then to make sure they were not followed. Not until they had put several miles between them and the ominous forest, did he really relax.

When they arrived at the sheriff's office, late in the afternoon, giving no heed to the curious crowd that followed at a respectful distance, they found a man awaiting them.

"Hello, Jeff," the sheriff greeted him. "Thought maybe you'd be here. Want you to know Walt Slade, a friend of mine."

Dunlap Jefferson certainly did not look the part of the irascible old shorthorn Sheriff Colton and Jim Hogg had intimated. He was not very tall, and slender. His features were smooth, almost cameo-perfect

in their regularity, his smile of acknowledge-
ment pleasant. But his eyes were like splinters of sapphire in his deeply bronzed face.
As he acknowledged the introduction, his
voice was soft and cultured. When he shook
hands with a firm grip, Slade sensed the
steel in the man.

A cold man with a passion, he diagnosed
Dunlap Jefferson.

The sheriff instructed a deputy who was
present to deliver the bodies to the coroner's
office, which was in the same building. Jefferson sat silently until the door closed on
the deputy. Then he remarked,

"So they got poor Cliff."

"Yes, somebody got him," acceded the
sheriff.

"Not much doubt as to who was behind
his killing."

"Perhaps, but there's no proof the oil
people had anything to do with it," the
sheriff replied, searching the other's face
with his gaze.

Dunlap Jefferson shrugged. His face
remained expressionless.

"Suppose you tell me how it happened,"
he suggested.

The sheriff gestured to Slade. "You tell
him," he said.

Slade proceeded to do so, leaving out no

detail of what he saw and experienced. Jefferson listened intently without interruption.

"And you got one of them," he observed, when Slade paused. *El Halcon* nodded.

"Now tell him about what happened today," the sheriff prodded.

Again Jefferson listened without comment until Slade again paused. Then he nodded his finely-shaped head, the dark hair of which was liberally shot with gray.

"A hard bunch, and smart," he said. "But that's to be expected."

Slade felt that Jefferson and the sheriff would like to discuss matters alone, so he rose to his feet.

"I'm going to the Crosby House for something to eat," he told Colton. "I'll be available whenever you want me for the inquest."

"Okay," nodded the sheriff. "I'll keep in touch with you."

"Good afternoon, Mr. Slade," said Jefferson. "I'll be seeing you again."

"Quite likely," Slade agreed, and departed.

"A capable appearing young fellow," Jefferson remarked after the door had closed.

"He's all of that," agreed the sheriff.

"And you don't recognize him?"

"Recognize him?"

"That's what I said. Tom, that man is *El Halcon*."

The sheriff's jaw sagged. *"El Halcon!"* he repeated incredulously.

"Yes," said Jefferson. "I saw him once, over at Corpus Christi, and once you see him you don't forget him. Plenty of folks will tell you he's the shrewdest and most dangerous outlaw in Texas. He prowls all over the state, and wherever he shows up there's trouble."

"Trouble for the wrong sort of people, I'd say from what I've seen of him in action," the sheriff replied grimly. "He saved my life, and no matter who or what he is, I'm for him so long as it is humanly possible for me to be for him."

Jefferson did not appear surprised, merely nodded. "Don't suppose you have any reward notices for him?"

Sheriff Colton snorted his disgust. "If you know anything about *El Halcon,* you'll know there are no reward notices out for him, and never have been so far as I've been able to learn, and it's my business to keep posted on such matters."

"He has killings to his credit, quite a few of them, I understand."

"To his credit is right," retorted the

sheriff. "The sort he's killed sure appeared to have a killing coming, and last night and today are no exceptions."

"You're prejudiced in the fellow's favor," said Jefferson, a note of exasperation creeping into his voice.

"If he'd kept you from eating lead, maybe you'd be a mite prejudiced too," returned the sheriff.

"Any idea why he's in this section?" asked Jefferson.

"No," replied the sheriff. "Have you?"

"Yes, I think I have," said Jefferson. "I think the oil people brought him here to do their gunslinging for them."

"I doubt it," grunted the sheriff.

"Well, I don't," snapped Jefferson, his voice hardening. "I've been in town since early morning and did quite a bit of scouting around. I was curious about the man who brought Cliff's body in and naturally asked questions. After I learned what I did, I was even more curious about him."

"What did you learn?" asked the sheriff.

"I learned that he had a long talk in the lobby of the Crosby House last night with — Jim Hogg!"

"Jim Hogg's an honest man," observed the sheriff.

"He is," agreed Jefferson, "but he has his

interests and the interests of his colleagues to consider. Hogg sets up to become a millionaire; chances are, he will. And with men like Gates and Cullinan and Swayne, business is business."

"They have a right to protect their interests."

"Yes, but not at the expense of the interests of others," said Jefferson. Abruptly his face darkened and his eyes caught the light like agate.

"About the only way to have peace and justice here is to clean out the whole nest of snakes," he declared, "and I've a good notion to do it."

The sheriff let his gaze rest on the other's face. "Listen, Jeff," he said, "you've been good to me; you swung votes my way in the election. But I'm a duly-elected peace officer, elected by the people of this county, and sworn to do my duty as a peace officer. I intend to do it, and I won't stand for anything like what you suggest. Don't try it!"

"I suppose the fact that the oil people will be able to swing a lot of votes has nothing to do with it," Jefferson said, with a sneer.

"It does not," answered Colton. "To tell the truth, I don't think I'll run again. I've had enough. I'm very much of the notion that I'll go back to following a cow's tail, where I can have peace and nothing to worry about. Being a sheriff ain't no bed of roses. Try to do the right thing and all you get is abuse from the folks who are supposed to be your friends. Yes, I've had enough."

Jefferson's face mirrored concern. "Hold on, Tom!" he exclaimed. "I didn't mean it the way you took it. I'm sorry. You mustn't pull out. If you do, they'll put in their own man, sure as shooting, and we'll end up being hogtied."

"I don't think you'd have to worry, if you didn't do something you ought not to," replied the sheriff. Nevertheless he looked somewhat mollified.

"Let's go across the street and have a drink," he suggested. "Maybe that'll help us both cool off."

After finishing his meal, Slade sat in the lobby of the Crosby House smoking and endeavoring to analyze and correlate the tumultuous happenings of the past twenty-four hours. Dunlap Jefferson, embroiled in a feud with the oil people, had disagreed, perhaps quarreled, with his range boss Cliff Tevis, who disapproved of the business. Then Tevis was run down and murdered by

51

a mounted band, two members of which rode horses bearing Jefferson's Diamond brand. Didn't seem logical that such a disagreement would afford the basis of the cold-blooded killing of a man who had worked for Jefferson for a long period of time and for whom the ranchowner apparently had a high respect. That is, on the face of what was known by Sheriff Colton. But there could have been threats involved, which decided Jefferson that Tevis knew too much, was a menace and had to be removed. Supposition, nothing more; no proof. And a rather too obvious explanation of Cliff Tevis' murder. Slade had learned to regard the obvious with suspicion.

All in all, what had set out to be a routine ranger chore had developed into something quite different and much more complex. Captain McNelty had sent him to Beaumont to investigate and break up, if possible, an outlaw band that had been harassing the section, and against which the local authorities appeared to be powerless.

"Just a regulation brushpoppin' outfit, the chances are," Captain Jim told his lieutenant. "Mosey down there and see what you can do with the horned toads. Usually something like that builds up wherever there's a strike, whether it's gold, oil, or what have you."

Something had built up, all right, but Slade was already pretty well convinced that something more than a "brushpopping" bunch was operating in the section. A shrewd outfit with a shrewd man at their head appeared to be more like it. The bank robbery and the payroll robberies had been big business. Perhaps in the beginning the object of the Twilight Riders had been to harass the oil operations, but evidently it didn't take them long to branch out to a field where the pickings were bigger. If Dunlap Jefferson had hired a bunch to assist him in his campaign against the oil field, the rapscallions had quickly gotten out of hand, which was to be expected. And apparently somebody was able to obtain information not open to the general public. Witness the wrecked train carrying payroll money from Port Arthur. Without a doubt the subterfuge had been a closely guarded secret, or was supposed to have been. The fact remained that the outlaws had learned about it, with resulting robbery and murder.

Slade wondered what was the significance of the slain drygulcher who indubitably had spent a good deal of time around the oil field. One explanation, of course, was that he had been planted by Jefferson to get the lowdown on activities there and report back to his employer on opportunities for making moves against the oil people. Again only conjecture, but the angle was interesting. For so far, Dunlap Jefferson was the only possible suspect.

However, Slade felt he hadn't done so bad during his brief sojourn in the section. He had eliminated two of the Twilight Riders, which was more than anybody else had so far managed to do. That is, conceding that the band which killed Cliff Tevis were the Riders. Slade hoped so. Two such bands operating in the section would be a little too much for comfort.

Leaving the Crosby House, he returned to the sheriff's office. Neither Sheriff Colton nor Dunlap Jefferson was there, but a deputy informed him that the inquest would be held the following morning at ten o'clock.

"The Old Man sure has taken a shine to you, feller," the deputy observed. "I heard him tell Jefferson that no matter who you were or what you were, he was for you till the last cow comes home."

"Nice of him," Slade smiled. "Hope I won't disappoint him."

"I don't think you will," said the deputy, casting an admiring glance at The Hawk's tall form. "I've a notion you don't disappoint folks over much. That is," he added, "unless they're the sort that have got a disappointment coming."

Slade chuckled at the deputy's quaint phraseology, told him "so long," and sauntered out to look the town over.

It was worth looking over, all right, for although it was hardly dusk, Beaumont's night life was already getting underway. The street was crowded with a motley throng of humanity. Brawny oil workers in greasy overalls and high-laced boots rubbed shoulders with lithe cowhands from the neighborhood spreads. There were Mexicans in black velvet adorned with much silver, as were their steeple-crowned sombreros. Colored folks, their teeth shining white in their black faces, chattered merrily as they jostled along. Here and there was a Chinese, and an occasional Indian. There were well-dressed shopkeepers. Gamblers in somber black save for the snow of their ruffled shirt fronts, "ladies" of the dance halls with lips that were just a trifle too red, eyes just a trifle too bright.

And it seemed to Slade that each and every one had but a single ambition, to get drunk as quickly and as thoroughly as possible. The bars were packed. Over the swinging doors came a babble of whirling words, song, or what was apparently intended for it, the cheerful chink of bottle necks on glass rims, and the ring of gold pieces on the "mahogany." Roulette wheels whirred, dice skipped across the green cloth like spotty-eyed evils, cards slithered in the hands of busy dealers. From the dance floors came the solid thump of boots and the sprightly click of high heels. The short and spangled skirts of the girls swirled wide in a coruscating glitter. Guitars strummed softly, violins whined, banjos plunked. All in all, it was a payday night in a Border cowtown or gold camp. Only every night was a "payday night" for Beaumont as "black gold" flowed from the wells in a steady stream. Beaumont was a bonanza town, making the most of the present, forgetting the past and heedless of the future.

After sauntering around a while, Slade entered a saloon diagonally across the street from the sheriff's office. It was quieter than most and the clientele appeared somewhat above the average. A really good orchestra conducted by a tall and dignified Mexican was playing soft music.

Glancing about, Slade saw Sheriff Colton and Dunlap Jefferson seated at a table near the orchestra stand. The sheriff spotted him and beckoned.

Slade crossed the room to the table.

"Draw up a chair, Mr. Slade, and have a drink," Jefferson invited pleasantly. "Tom and I are relaxing a bit after a hard day."

"Thanks," Slade accepted, dropping into a chair. "Guess I can stand one."

"I imagine you can — several, after what you've been through during the past twenty-four hours," Jefferson said with a smile.

At the moment, the orchestra leader happened to glance in that direction. He started visibly and a pleased smile overspread his swarthy countenance.

"This is Terry Sullivan's place — it's called 'Sullivan's,' " remarked the sheriff. "Everything on the up-and-up here, including the games and the gals. Good place to keep in mind when you don't feel like being bothered with having to keep your eyes skun all the time. More than can be said for most of the rumholes in this pueblo. Some nice places, but a lot of others will take the gold fillings out of your teeth so slick you won't miss 'em."

Slade smiled and raised his glass, showing even teeth that flashed startlingly white in his bronzed face. He turned at a touch on his shoulder.

The orchestra leader was standing beside

him, smiling. *"Capitan,"* he said, employing the Mexican title of respect, *"Capitan,* will you not sing for us? I heard you once and I do not forget. It will be the great pleasure for all."

Slade, still smiling, was about to shake his head when Dunlap Jefferson touched his arm.

"Mr. Slade," he said, "I love good music, and if Miguel asks you to sing, you must be good, for he's no snide himself. I would consider it a great favor if you would sing."

"Okay," Slade acceded, "if the crowd doesn't object."

The smile abruptly left Miguel's black eyes and was replaced by a hard glitter.

"None will object, of that I give the promise," he said. "Come, *Capitan,* to the dais."

"He's a tough customer when you get him started, is Miguel, and Sullivan backs him to the hilt," murmured the sheriff as the leader turned away.

Slade arose and sauntered to the little raised platform which accommodated the orchestra and accepted a guitar that Miguel handed him with a low bow. The leader stepped to the edge of the platform and raised his hand. His voice rang out, clear and penetrating.

"*Senores* and *senoritas,*" he called. "We will have the silence, please. I, for you, have the great treat. My *amigo, El Capitan,* will sing for us."

The babble of talk died to a drone as all eyes turned expectantly to the tall man on the edge of the platform. Slade ran his slim fingers over the strings of the guitar with crisp power, played a masterly prelude. Then he threw back his black head and sang — sang a rollicking old ballad of the range. And as the great metallic baritone-bass pealed and thundered under the low ceiling, a hush fell over the room. Drinks stood forgotten on the bar. The dealers ceased to deal. The dancers paused. The orchestra leader stood smiling proudly.

With a crash of chords the music ended. For a moment, the silence endured. Then came a roar of applause and shouts of, "Give us another, feller! Give us another!"

The strings of the guitar whispered softly, and again the glorious golden voice rang out in a song beloved by the *peons* of *Mejico,* the humble people of the soil, pouring forth the touching beauty of their earthiness, their regrets for all things not done well, their dreams of that which can never be, their submissive acceptance of that which is, and the soaring hope of the meek and lowly.

The orchestra leader brushed the cuff of his velvet jacket across his eyes. The dance floor girls let the tears fall unashamed as they gazed at the smiling-eyed singer of dreams standing straight and tall in his youth and strength. And Jefferson sat as a man entranced, his eyes softening, his expression rapt.

One last breath of exquisite melody and Slade handed the guitar back to the leader, who brokenly murmured a word of thanks.

"Any doubt in your mind now as to whether he's *El Halcon*?" Jefferson asked the sheriff. "The singingest man in the whole Southwest, he's called."

"And the best shot and the fastest on the draw," added the sheriff. "Yep, I guess he's all three."

FIVE

As Slade returned to the table he saw a huge red-haired man with twinkling dark eyes standing beside the sheriff. He rightly guessed it was Terry Sullivan, the owner.

"Mr. Slade," Jefferson said, "I'd be glad to pay you tophand wages just to hang around and sing for me."

"Oh, no, you won't," broke in Terry Sullivan. "I'll overbid anything you offer. If I had him here, I wouldn't have to bother to sell whiskey. Folks would pack the place every night just to hear him sing."

"A mite of exaggeration on the part of both of you, I fear, gentlemen, but thanks for the compliment," Slade said as he sat down.

"Not a bit of it," declared Sullivan. He beckoned a waiter. "On the house," he said, "and keep 'em coming. Maybe you might be after singing us another one after a while," he remarked insinuatingly to Slade.

"Perhaps if I drop in later," Slade promised. "I must leave shortly. Have an appointment at the Crosby House in about twenty minutes."

Jefferson shot the sheriff a quick glance. Slade noticed, and bit back a grin with difficulty.

When Slade arrived at the Crosby House he failed to see Jim Hogg in the lobby. A moment later, however, the headwaiter was beside him, bowing.

"This way, Mr. Slade," he said. "Mr. Hogg is awaiting you in the dining room."

He led the way to a table where the ex-governor was seated. With him was a tall, well-set up, youngish looking man with keen, pale eyes and an urbane manner.

"Hello, Walt," Hogg greeted. "Sit down and eat. This is Mr. Berne Rader, who is interested in oil. Rader, meet Mr. Walt Slade, a friend of mine."

Rader rose and offered his hand. "Anybody who is a friend of Mr. Hogg's is a friend of mine," he declared. "How are you, Mr. Slade?"

It was some hours since Slade had eaten and with the healthy appetite of youth and vigorous living, he enjoyed an excellent dinner. Hogg ordered drinks and they settled down to smoke and talk.

"Interested in the oil business, Mr. Slade?" Rader asked.

"Not particularly, but I find it interesting," Slade replied.

"Too darn interesting at times," grumbled Hogg. "You don't know which end you're standing on, and this town is bedlam. Take your life in your hands whenever you venture on the streets after dark. The town marshal tells you to walk in the middle of the street after nightfall and to tote guns. Says to tote 'em in your hands and not on your hips, so everybody can see you're loaded."

"It'll quiet down before long," Rader predicted cheerfully. "The unscrupulous always find smooth going for a time after a strike, but they never corral anything of importance. They'll fade out of the picture soon and reputable businessmen will take over and lift Beaumont out of the boom-day madness and stabilize the oil industry."

"I hope you're right," said Hogg. "Gates and Swayne will be here shortly, Walt," he added. "They're upstairs arguing with Jim Roche over an option. You'll like Roche. He's an Englishman, and a soldier of fortune. He's got a head on his shoulders, and has been around plenty."

Rader looked at his watch. "Got to be trailing my twine," he said. "Have an appointment."

With a nod and a smile he left the room, walking with a quick, smooth stride.

"Berne's a speculator," remarked Hogg. "Been mixed up in a lot of things — lumber, cotton, rice, and now oil. Owns stock in the Port Arthur railroad and is on the board of directors. Comes from Louisiana. Well recommended."

"Talks more like a Texan," Slade observed.

"Come to think of it, he does," Hogg agreed. "Been around over here a lot, I suppose. Here come Roche and the others."

Slade did like Roche, the quiet, dignified Englishman whose handsome face, despite his keenness, wore a dreamy expression. He also liked Swayne and "Bet-a-Million" Gates. The genial Swayne looked the part of the successful businessman that he was. Gates had merry, reckless eyes and a ready sense of humor. Like Hogg, there was nothing pretentious about the three of them. They were unassuming men with a keen zest for life and any game that required daring and promised competition.

After a couple of drinks, Gates' habitual restlessness manifested itself.

"Let's take a walk and look things over a

bit," he suggested. "Getting stuffy in here."

"You're never satisfied unless you're nosing into something that may make for trouble," grumbled Hogg. "Oh, all right. If we all get shot, don't blame me."

"I think Mr. Slade will be able to protect us," chuckled Gates. "He looks competent."

Many eyes watched them leave the hotel and heads drew together in speculation.

"I like this town," said Gates. "It's lively and rambunctious. Bet you a million something blows sky high before the night is over."

Gates proved a true prophet, but not in the manner he anticipated. They were strolling along Crockett Street when from the south came a rumbling boom. They turned to stare in the direction of the sound. For some minutes they gazed in silence. However, the sound was not repeated.

"That was a dynamite explosion, or I miss my guess," Gates finally observed. "Bet you a million another derrick has gone to glory. Aren't those scoundrels ever going to let up?"

"Seems quiet enough down there now," remarked Swayne.

"But it isn't," Slade said. "Look!" Again the others stared, muttering under their breath. A reddish glow was spreading along the horizon, creeping up the long slant of the sky, pulsing, deepening, growing brighter and brighter.

"Hoppin' horn toads!" exclaimed Hogg. "That's a fire, sure as blazes! A big one, too!"

"And that other thing sure was a dynamite explosion," added Gates. "Let's go down there and see what's going on. We can get horses at the hotel livery stable. You'll come along, Mr. Slade?"

"Yes," *El Halcon* replied. "I'll meet you in front of the hotel." He turned and hurried to the stable where Shadow was stalled.

Fifteen minutes later they rode south at a fast pace, and they didn't ride alone. It seemed half the population of Beaumont was streaming south, via horseback or on foot. The sky was now blood-red, with flickering streamers of light running to the zenith.

"It's a well, all right," jolted Swayne. "Looks like it's right in the middle of the field. This could be serious."

As they drew nearer the conflagration, Slade felt that Swayne's remark was very much of an underestimate. The burning well was surrounded by a forest of derricks. However, there was little wind and so far the fire hadn't spread. Other explosions were rocking the air, accompanied by yellow flashes.

"They're trying to cave in the well with dynamite," said Hogg, "but I guess they can't get close enough to toss one down the bore because of the heat."

Even as they reached the vicinity, the derrick, its supporting timbers burned through, toppled and fell with a thunderous crash, flinging sparks and burnings brands in every direction, driving back the workers who were trying frantically to extinguish the fire.

Slade studied the sky. High, fleecy clouds were hurrying across the face of the moon.

"There's wind coming in from the Gulf," he said to Hogg. "High so far, but it's very liable to drop."

"If it does, the whole blasted field will go up in smoke," Hogg predicted grimly. "Those fellows aren't making any headway at all."

As they drew rein, Slade scanned the well and its surroundings, estimated the breadth of the soaring flames.

"It's a gassy one and the pressure shoots the fire high," he observed. Abruptly he turned to Jim Hogg.

"Have somebody get a hundred foot length of wire cable, heavy," he said. "I'll see what I can make of it."

"What do you aim to do?" Hogg asked.

"Fasten a bundle of capped and fused dynamite sticks to one end of the cable and draw it across the well," Slade replied. "That way I can dump the sticks down the bore and cave in the well and put out the fire."

"A hundred feet of heavy steel cable!" exclaimed Hogg. "Man, you could never pull it, and even if you could, you couldn't get close enough to that fire to grab the end. You'd be only about fifty feet from the well."

"I think I can," Slade replied.

"But when the dynamite lets go, it will blow you to kingdom come," protested Hogg.

"I'll chance it," Slade replied. "Give the orders."

"I always knew Jim McNelty was loco as a coot and I guess like attracts like," Hogg sputtered in low tones and began bellowing orders to men in authority about the well.

Very quickly, the materials were assembled. The cable was stretched out parallel to the well at a safe distance, the dynamite attached. Overhead the clouds were thickening and the first faint breath of the dropping wind could be felt.

"No time to lose," Slade said. He stationed his companions to relay the signal to light the fuse when he gave the order. The dynamite was moved as close to the thundering well as the blistering heat would permit.

"Holy smoke!" panted Gates. "Even here it's hotter'n blazes. Slade, you'll be as scorched as Judas Iscariot!"

"Or blown higher than the Tower of Babel," observed Swayne.

The quiet Roche spoke for the first time. "I'll go with you and help pull it," he offered.

Slade smilingly shook his head. "Thanks," he said, "but I'll do better by myself and have a better chance to get in the clear when the blow comes. Two men are liable to get in each other's way. All set? Here we go!"

The task to which Slade had set himself was indeed an herculean one. The hundred feet of steel cable was a tremendous weight for one man to drag over the rough ground; and to obtain the proper angle to draw the dynamite across the well meant that he must pass within fifty feet or less of the roaring fire. An additional hazard — should the gas pressure in the well lower even a little, the flames would instantly spread out and he would be burned to a crisp.

Gripping the noose he had twisted in the cable with both hands, he ran diagonally toward the well. The heat struck him like the draft from a blast furnace, with its choking fumes from the burning gas. He gasped for breath, coughing; and this was nothing to what was to come. He shot a swift glance over his shoulder, estimating the angle. Half-turning, he signaled to Jim Hogg, who at once passed the word to the others to light the fuse.

Back came the signal along the line of watchers. Slade tightened his grip on the cable and hurled himself forward, slanting toward the well. Once the cable was across the well mouth, he would have to work fast or the intense heat would burn even the heavy wire in two. The crater was wide now, and widening more by the second, the casing and flow-pipe having long since melted, leaving only the naked earth to crumble under the onslaught of the flames. Nearer and nearer the fire he drew as the angle became more acute. The heat was withering, seeming to dry the blood in his veins. His eyelashes were beginning to feel sticky. His shirt was smoldering. Now he was less than fifty feet from the sluffing-off edge of the well. Casting a glance over his shoulder, he ran a few more steps along the diagonal.

To the tense watchers at a safe distance from the impending explosion, it seemed that he was at the very edge of the flame-spouting well. Gates was swearing softly under his breath. Jim Hogg clenched his fists till his nails drew blood from his palms.

"He can never do it!" gulped Swayne. "Damn it! We shouldn't have let him go. No man living can pull that cable across the well."

"Don't be too sure," cautioned Roche. "Look! He's straightening out for the pull."

"And he looks like he's ready to fall," growled Gates, still swearing.

Slade was in trouble. He could stand no more. If this wouldn't do it, his expedient was a failure. Another step nearer that inferno and he'd tumble over, which would mean the end of the well and him also, and very likely the whole Spindletop field, for the wind was rising swiftly, the crest of the flames wavering and bending northward. Another swift glance and he darted forward, turning away from the fire. He thought he felt a slight jerk on the taut line of steel, which should mean that the end and the dynamite bundle had dropped down the bore, although it could also only mean that the cable was sagging as it stretched across the crater. His senses whirling, he stumbled on, slowly now, for the cable seemed to have caught on something and the drag on his aching arms was terrific. His great desire was to drop the humming line, ease the strain on muscles that were turning to water, and flee madly from this hell of heat and exhaustion. He grimly set his teeth and staggered on.

At that instant the explosion came. A thundering bellow that dwarfed the roar of the burning well. Slade was hurled through the air by the concussion; he thought he would never come down.

He did, finally, with a thud, sprawling on all fours, flattening out with a force that drove the breath from his lungs and sent red flashes storming before his eyes. About him rained flaming timbers, clots of fire, and other debris that pounded the ground with pile-driver blows. A hunk of something ripped the flesh of his upper arm and the pain licked back the wave of unconsciousness that was flowing over him. With a mighty effort he scrambled to his feet and staggered forward blindly.

Curious how still it had suddenly become. Still, save for somebody yelling something. Quite a lot of somebodies. What a racket they were making! Why? Abruptly he realized that hands were gripping his arms, rushing him ahead. And that the racket which annoyed him was cheer after cheer that rang to the cloudy heavens.

"You did it!" whooped a voice that was

vaguely familiar. "Son, you did it! The bore's caved in, the fire's out! You did it! Blazes! What a man!"

"Easy, Gates, easy," cautioned another familiar voice. "Don't you see he's out on his feet? Give me that flask, Roche; a pull at it ought to help."

Slade realized that the neck of a bottle was being pressed to his lips, liquid running into his mouth. He swallowed convulsively and the stuff ran through his veins like liquid fire.

"Nothing like good old tequila to snap a feller out of it," chuckled the voice that he now recognized as belonging to Jim Hogg. "Easy, that's enough, you'll choke him."

When Slade came back to something like normal, he found he was sitting on a timber with Hogg and Gates hovering over him, a crowd of jabbering oil workers pressing close.

"Rather silly of me to pass out that way," he remarked with a wan smile.

"Silly!" snorted Jim Hogg. "It's a wonder to me you didn't drop dead! And the way the wind's rising, I've a notion you saved the whole blasted field from going up in smoke, every derrick, every building. Spindletop would have had to start over from scratch. Say! There's blood on your

73

arm! You're hurt!"

"Just a scratch," Slade replied. "Guess I should be grateful to whatever hit me. The sting of it snapped me awake as I was going under."

"Let's have a look," said Hogg. He examined the ragged cut. "Have it taken care of right away," he said. "Nothing bad, but it shouldn't be neglected. We'll rout out a doctor soon as we get back to town."

"First," Slade said, rising to his feet, "first, let's try and find where that initial explosion was set off."

"Why, it was here at the well, wasn't it?" said Swayne.

Slade shook his head. "You don't fire a well with dynamite," he replied. "That would just ruin the derrick and cave in the bore. That blast was a decoy set to attract everybody's attention and give the hellions a chance to do their chore. A little work with a drill and an electric spark was all that was needed."

"It was over at the west edge of the field, sir," a voice cried. "An old abandoned well and derrick. We all ran over there to see what was going on. Guess everybody was looking that way."

"As they were intended to," Slade nodded. "Let's go there."

When they reached the scene of the explosion, Slade went over the ground carefully with the aid of a lantern. Quickly he noted what everybody else overlooked — the prints of high bootheels in the soft soil. Prints left by two men, he concluded. He decided not to mention his discovery to his companions.

As they walked back to their horses, Jim Hogg remarked,

"You made a lot of friends tonight, Slade, but I'm afraid you also made some bad enemies. The skunks who fired that well won't feel kind toward you. I've a notion you'd better keep your eyes skinned if you happen to be riding the rangeland in this section."

"So you're convinced that the cattlemen are responsible," Slade answered.

"Who else, will you tell me?" Hogg snorted.

"I can't, not at present, at least," Slade admitted. He was suffering a little disquietude himself, for he kept recalling the prints made by high-heel boots such as no oil worker ever wore.

When they reached the Crosby House, Hogg insisted in arousing a doctor who roomed there and having the cut in Slade's arm attended to.

"Can't afford to take chances with you," he declared. "Liable to need you any time."

When they were alone at a table, enjoying a snack, Gates and the others having paused to greet some acquaintances at the bar, Hogg let out a chuckle.

"Did you hear Swayne ranting about how Jim McNelty hasn't answered the letter he wrote him asking for a troop of rangers? Guess Swayne would be a mite surprised if he knew the facts."

"The way things are working out, Captain Jim may have to do just that," Slade replied, a trifle grimly. "He didn't envision such conditions as exist here when he sent me alone."

"I don't think he will," Hogg disagreed cheerfully. "I have every confidence in your ability to handle the situation."

"Hope you're right," said Slade. "Well, I'm going to call it a night. Been sort of a hectic day, and I'm due at the inquest at ten in the morning. Be seeing you."

"Goodnight, Walt," said the former governor. "Take care of yourself, and thanks for everything. We won't forget it."

Six

The inquest the following morning was short, the jury's verdict also short and to the point. Cliff Tevis met his death at the hands of parties unknown, it said, and the sheriff was advised to run the sidewinders down as quickly as possible. The two drygulchers got what was coming to them. Slade was commended for having done a good chore.

Sheriff Colton, a witness, and Dunlap Jefferson were present at the inquest. After the hearing was over they approached Slade.

"How are you this morning, Mr. Slade?" the latter greeted him. "My offer of last night still stands. Everybody is singing your praises," he added with a wry smile. "It was an admirable piece of work, but what you should have done was let the whole stinking mess go up in smoke. Then perhaps we would have had peace again hereabouts."

"Nothing permanent would have been accomplished," Slade replied. "It would merely have been a temporary setback for the oil people. You can't stop the wheels of progress, Mr. Jefferson."

"Maybe not, but a little sand in the gears now and then can slow 'em up," Jefferson retorted grimly. "Drop over to my place when you have time. I understand you also play the piano, and I have a good one."

"I'll do that, sir," Slade promised, and meant it. He was more than a little curious about Dunlap Jefferson, especially after his remark anent his piano playing. It would appear Jefferson knew more about *him* than he had surmised. He wondered where the ranchowner got his information.

Cliff Tevis' body, intended for burial at the Diamond ranch, was placed in a light wagon which had been brought to town by several of the Diamond hands. An average bunch of rannies, Slade thought, and liked their looks. They appeared genuinely grieved at the death of their range boss and bitter against his slayers. They approached Slade in a group, shook hands with him and thanked him for bringing in Tevis' body.

"Pity you didn't get more of the skunks," remarked a grizzled bowleg named Rafferty. "Better luck next time, and I hope I'll be along to lend a hand. Ride over and see us, feller, we'll be glad to have you.

"And I've a notion the boss, Mr. Jefferson, has took a shine to you," he added confidentially. "A good man to work for; you could do worse than tie up with him."

Slade was not at all certain about the "shine," but he was willing to agree that Dunlap Jefferson was doubtless a good man to work for. Most oldtime cowmen were.

"Well, what do you think?" the sheriff asked after Jefferson and his hands had departed with the corpse.

"I think that if those I saw are a fair sample of Jefferson's riders, they have nothing to do with any skulduggery that may be going on," Slade replied.

"And Jefferson?"

"As to Jefferson, I must hold my judgment in abeyance till I know more about him."

"Jeff is convinced that oil people brought you here."

"He may not be too far wrong," Slade replied, with a ghost of a smile.

Sheriff Colton looked puzzled, and tugged his mustache. "To do their gunslinging for them," he added abruptly.

"In that, he is definitely wrong," Slade answered, the smile broadening.

"Dadgum you! I don't know what to make

of you!" the sheriff exclaimed querulously.

Slade laughed outright. That laugh was infectious and the sheriff had to grin, albeit dourly.

"First, you save my life at the risk of your own. The minute you took to slap me down out of range of that sidewinder's bullet might have meant you'd get it," he said. "Then you go and save their field for the oil people, and again risked your life to do it. You just about hypnotized Jeff with your singing, and you hadn't talked a minute at the inquest till you had the whole jury on your side. No, I don't know what to make of you."

Slade laughed again; the sheriff's bewilderment was really comical.

"I think I'll mosey down to the field and look things over," he said.

"Go ahead, if you can stand it," replied the sheriff. "Be seeing you."

Before he had ridden a quarter of a mile, Slade's olfactory nerves were assailed by a heavy, dank odor. Shadow sneezed, and snorted his distaste.

"Feller, you haven't smelled anything yet," Slade told him. "Just wait till you get close."

Slade could feel a certain sympathy for the cattlemen, having the clean air of the rangeland so tainted, which fostered the superstition that cows were killed by the oil fumes. He was not particularly fond of it himself.

The field was a scene of hectic activity. All was bustle and orderly confusion. A crew was busy at work re-opening the caved-in bore of the well which was fired the night before. They recognized Slade and shouted greetings, which he answered with a wave of his hand. He pulled Shadow to a halt and sat gazing over the forest of derricks that bristled up in every direction. Spindletop was a big one, all right, and growing bigger all the time.

"The time is coming, horse, when oil will produce more Texas wealth than cattle or anything else," he predicted to Shadow, who looked dubious and was still not favorably impressed.

Rolling a cigarette and hooking one long leg over the saddle horn, Slade sat at his ease and surveyed the roar and clatter and the tumult and the shouting that was Spindletop. The massive walking beams jigged their unceasing see-saw dance. The cables rose and fell as the ponderous steel bits drove deep into the earth to tap anew the great subterranean pool of "black gold" that the slow and subtle chemistry of Nature had created during untold epochs of time.

Capped wells flowed their never-ending streams into the pipes which conveyed it to the huge storage tanks that sprouted on the prairie like gigantic mushrooms. Soon a pipeline, already under construction, would reach Port Arthur, where the oil could take to the sea for the marts of all the bright water ports of the world.

Progress! Slade mused. You can't stop it. Those who try are just so many pigmy Canutes trying to sweep back the ocean tide with a broom. But somebody was liable to get "drowned" in the process. He was here to try and prevent too many "drownings." But how the devil was he to do it? He didn't know, yet.

He circled the field and then rode west for some miles across land he knew to be part of Dunlap Jefferson's holdings. As he rode he studied the terrain with the eye of an engineer and a geologist. Finally he turned and gazed long and earnestly at the dark smudge staining the clear blue of the sky which marked the site of the field.

"Could be," he observed cryptically to Shadow. "Yes, could be, if a subterranean slope much lower than that which bottoms the Spindletop pool happens to be reversed. Something to consider, horse, something to consider. Let's head for town."

After stabling Shadow and making sure all his wants were provided against, Slade repaired to his room in the Crosby House and freshened up a bit. When he descended to the lobby, the headwaiter was almost instantly at his side, bowing deferentially.

"Mr. Hogg and Mr. Gates are at their table and would welcome your company, sir," he said. "This way, if you please."

The two oil magnates greeted Slade with enthusiasm. "Figured you'd be showing up about now and told Henry to be on the lookout for you," said Hogg. "Sit down and join us in a bite. Heard you were down at the field, looking things over. What do you think of it?"

"I found it quite interesting," Slade replied as he sat down.

"Yes, yes, it's all of that, even to one with little technical knowledge of such matters," Gates said in his queer, jerky manner of speaking.

Jim Hogg, who knew about all there was to know about Walt Slade, stifled a grin.

"I've a notion Walt will catch on fast," he said.

"I don't doubt it, I don't doubt it," agreed Gates. "The way he handled that situation last night proves it."

Slade enjoyed a good dinner and agreed

with Hogg that Gates, who handled that angle of the ordering, certainly knew good drinks from bad.

"I would say Mr. Gates is a connoisseur of fine brandy," he observed, inhaling the bouquet with appreciation.

Gates shot him a quick glance and his brows drew together slightly as in perplexity. A little later, when Slade left the table for a moment, he remarked querulously, "Can't make him out! Can't make him out! He looks and dresses like a cowboy, but he sure doesn't talk like one. Got me puzzled, and it's not often that somebody puzzles me."

"Not all cowhands are unlettered," Hogg returned. "You'll meet quite a few with a smattering of education."

"If he's a fair sample, they'd do well as college professors," Gates grunted.

Jim Hogg chuckled and the discussion ceased as Slade returned to the table.

When the meal was concluded, they sat together in the lobby for some time. Gates and Hogg discussed at length the ramifications of the oil business, while Slade smoked and listened. After a while, Gates' habitual restlessness manifested itself.

"Let's go over to Terry Sullivan's place," he suggested. "Big poker game there tonight, Berne Rader told me. Said he figured to sit in."

"Rader always figures to sit in where there's a game for high stakes," Hogg observed. "He can't leave cards alone. Usually wins, though. Sometimes gets sort of ugly if he loses, I've noticed."

"Cards are too slow, too slow," said Gates. "Take you forever to make a million that way. Let's go!"

Sullivan's was booming when they arrived. They quickly spotted the big game at a corner table; there were six players in all, including Berne Rader. Three were garbed in greasy overalls and oil-spotted shirts. Two, like Rader, were dressed conservatively and in good taste.

"Those fellers in the dirty clothes all own wells," Gates observed to Slade. "They'll end up doing okay, I figure. Right on the job at their bores all the time, doing their share of the chores and seeing that their men do theirs right, too. I don't know the other two jiggers; could be most anything. Must be well-heeled though, to sit in that game. Let's go over there."

With Gates leading, they crossed the room and took up places with other bystanders watching the big game.

"I think Rader's losing," Gates remarked

in low tones. "He looks it."

Slade regarded the speculator and was inclined to agree. Also, he concluded that Rader had the gambling fever, and had it bad. His face was flushed, his eyes glittering, and there was sweat on his upper lip. And he appeared to be in a thoroughly bad temper.

If Rader was losing, it was just as obvious that one of the well owners, seated across the table directly opposite him, was winning. There were huge stacks of chips in front of him, and as Slade and his companions watched, he raked in a big pot, to which Rader had contributed largely. He was a big man with a rather truculent look. The deal was going around and it was his turn to handle the cards. He proceeded to shuffle them, rather clumsily, taking his time about it. His deliberate movements irritated Rader, who kept muttering under his breath. Abruptly he burst into speech.

"For the love of Pete, deal, can't you!" he almost shouted. "If you can't, pass it to somebody who can, you blasted butterfingers!"

The oil man flushed darkly and his eyes snapped. "All right, you deal 'em!" he said, and threw the deck in Rader's face.

Rader reeled back, almost overturning his

chair. Then his right hand shot forward like the head of a striking snake. A wicked little double-barreled derringer spatted into his palm from a sleeve holster.

It seemed to the paralyzed watchers the draw and the blaze of the gun were simultaneous. But a split second before Rader pulled trigger, fingers like rods of woven steel clamped his wrist and jerked the muzzle up. The bullet thudded harmlessly into the far wall near the ceiling. Slade put forth his strength. Rader howled with pain as that terrible grip ground his wrist bones together. His nerveless fingers opened and the derringer thudded on the table. With another yell, he twisted about and launched a blow at Slade's face with his free hand.

Before it had traveled six inches it was blocked; then Slade had his other wrist and he was held helpless, cursing and fuming.

"Take it easy, Mr. Rader," Slade said quietly. "That would have been mighty close to a cold-blooded killing; the other man isn't even heeled, so far as I can see."

"That's right, Berne," Jim Hogg broke in. "When you cool down you'll be thanking Slade for what he did. If it hadn't been for him, right now you'd be in serious trouble. There's a limit to what you can get away with, even in a town like this."

The fire in Rader's eyes died. His face straightened out. "Guess you're right," he acceded. "Thanks, Mr. Slade." He turned his gaze on the well owner, who sat white and silent, in his eyes the look of a man who had just glanced across into eternity and saw it wasn't far.

"I'm sorry, Caldwell," he said. "Sorry I lost my temper, but that deck in my face hurt. I'm willing to forget it all, if you are. Here's my hand on it."

The two men shook hands and the game proceeded, very quietly.

Big Terry Sullivan was at Slade's side, wiping away the sweat that streamed down his face.

"And I want to say much obliged, too," he said. "That would have been bad, mighty bad, if it hadn't been for you. Blazes! I never saw anything so fast in my life! I'd have swore Caldwell was a goner."

"He came darn near being," grunted Hogg. "That blasted sleeve gun is a Forty-one and makes a mighty big hole at close range."

"I recall Roche saying last night that he figured Slade was very likely full of surprises. Guess he had the right idea. What next are you going to spring on us, son?"

"Have you ever heard him sing, Mr.

Gates?" asked Sullivan. "No? Then you're in for another surprise. Maybe he'll give us one later. Won't you, Mr. Slade?" he wheedled.

"Perhaps," Slade replied absently, for his thoughts were elsewhere.

The "gambler's draw," it's called, the expulsion, from a cleverly constructed holster in a coat sleeve, of the stubby little derringer with its lethal charge to the palm of the hand. The knack of which is acquired by dint of natural aptitude and much practice. A handy tool for a man who is sitting and has his hands occupied with cards. Slade had never seen the "draw" employed by anyone other than a professional gambler or dealer. Which lent, he thought, a peculiar interest to the recent episode.

Well, it wasn't so remarkable that Berne Rader might have been at one time a professional gambler or dealer. For a speculator was often as much a gambler as one who woos the goddess of chance via the pasteboards. Just a similar matter of out-guessing the other fellow, all the angles of the subject to hand explored as thoroughly as possible. With the same hazard that the other fellow may have an "ace" in the hole. Or, *sometimes*, one up his sleeve.

Slade and his companions moved away

and sat down at a table, leaving the subdued poker players to their game. Hogg shook his head.

"That temper of his will get Rader into real trouble sometime," he predicted. "Of course there was a certain amount of provocation, but certainly not enough to warrant a shooting."

Slade said nothing, but he reflected that the killer-type usually reaches for a weapon, and they are found in all walks of life. He felt that Dunlap Jefferson was very likely also one, more calculatingly and coldly so than the hot tempered Rader.

Slade was drawn from his abstractions by a shadow falling across the table. Miguel, the orchestra leader, was beside him, bowing and smiling, and holding forth a guitar.

"*El Capitan* will sing?" he pleaded.

"Go ahead, Mr. Slade," Gates said, as *El Halcon* hesitated. "Let's see if you can do something else better than anybody else."

So Slade sang for them, a gay ballad of the rangeland and a love song of old Spain.

"Didn't I tell you those jiggers would stop playing to listen?" chuckled Terry Sullivan.

The poker players had indeed forgotten their cards and the mountainous stacks of chips before them. All eyes were turned to the tall singer of dreams. Berne Rader's face wore the expression of a man struggling with memory, endeavoring to recall something that eludes him. Abruptly his eyes glowed. He leaned forward, staring at Slade, his lips moving in inaudible speech. Then he relaxed, sitting back in his chair; but his cold eyes never left Slade's face.

"I still can't make him out!" Bet-a-Million Gates complained. "Why the devil is a man with a voice like that riding the chuck line. Or working on a ranch, for that matter."

"Slade gets double pay for singing the cows to sleep," Jim Hogg replied without the trace of a smile. "Never a stampede when Slade is around."

Gates shot him a suspicious glance, but didn't argue the point.

"Betcha he could sing a rattlesnake outa fangin'," remarked Sullivan. "Or shoot its head off at twenty paces," he added reflectively.

With applause still shaking the room, Slade came back to the table to receive the compliments of his companions.

"Still full of surprises," said Gates. "You get more interesting all the time."

Slade smiled, but was not impressed. Nor was he at all satisfied with himself. Captain Jim didn't send him to the Beaumont country to sing songs or put out fires or hobnob with oil tycoons. Which, he told himself morosely, was about all he'd been doing of late. Well, maybe business would pick up soon. It was due to, very soon.

"Say!" Gates suddenly exclaimed. "There's a funny one; Rader is cashing in and leaving the game. He usually is right there till the last dog's dead."

Slade glanced at the poker table. Berne Rader was counting his chips and handing them to the house man. A few minutes later he received payment for them. He said a few words to his companions, rose to his feet and sauntered to Slade's table, where he paused.

"Got to catch an early train for Port Arthur," he said. "Have an appointment with a representative of the Kountz interests. Be seeing you, gents."

He sauntered out. Gates watched him go, a little pucker between his brows.

"I'd give a pretty to know what that slick article has up his sleeve," he muttered.

"The Kountz interests, the Sabine Pass promoters, opposed Arthur Stillwell's plan for the construction of docks and a ship canal handled by the Port Arthur Canal and Dock Company," he explained to Slade, who nodded, being familiar with the details of that promotion row between huge syndicates.

"In which outfit you have an interest," Hogg observed to Gates.

"That's right," the Wall Street man conceded. "And, naturally, I also have an interest in anything Rader contemplates arranging with the Kountz people.

"Guess most of this is gibberish to you, Mr. Slade," he remarked for *El Halcon's* benefit, "but it could be a serious matter where I'm concerned. The Kountz outfit delayed the construction of the canal by their manipulations, and they may attempt to divert the pipeline from its planned course. Of that I'm not sure, but forewarned is forearmed, which is why I'd like to know what Rader has in mind. He's shrewd and resourceful and, although I usually don't deal in gossip, I have at least a faint suspicion that he's not overly burdened with a conscience."

Slade nodded vaguely and let it go at that; but his keen mind was busy analyzing and evaluating what he had learned.

Jim Hogg looked at his watch. "I'm going to bed," he announced. "Was up early today. You fellows coming along?"

Gates nodded and stood up. Slade shook

his head. "Think I'll stick around for a while," he said.

When the oil magnates had departed, Slade rolled a cigarette and sat watching the dancers, thinking. A little later a man entered the saloon, glanced about inquiringly and approached Slade's table.

"Mr. Slade, isn't it?" he asked. "I'm Handley, one of Sheriff Colton's deputies. He told me to ask you if you would step over to his office for a few minutes? It's right across the street, you know."

"Certainly," Slade agreed, rising to his feet. The messenger smiled and nodded and headed for the bar. Slade went across the street to the sheriff's office. As he mounted the steps he glanced through the open window. A low-turned bracket lamp burned behind the desk and he could see the old peace officer slumping back in his chair, his eyes closed, apparently in sleep. Slade pushed open the door, which stood ajar, stepped through — and looked squarely into the muzzle of a gun!

SEVEN

"Up!" said the man behind the gun, a thickset individual whose eyes glinted in the shadow of his hatbrim. "Easy! I know your reputation for fast gunslinging. One move and you get it."

Slade raised his hands; there was nothing else to do. He was caught settin'. The gunman moved back a couple of steps and to one side, his eyes never leaving Slade.

"Come ahead," he ordered. "That's enough. Dirk, get his hardware."

A second man, long and lanky, stepped from the shadows and plucked Slade's Colts from their holsters and shoved them under his own belt. The gun holder moved a little more to the side.

"Right through the back door," he said, "and keep on moving till I tell you to stop. I'll be right behind you, and my finger's itchin'. Oh, don't worry about him," he added as Slade glanced at the motionless form of the sheriff. "Just a little whack on the head to keep him quiet. He'll be coming out of it soon. We sorta used him for bait, you see."

As he moved ahead as ordered, Slade reflected it was a well-baited trap, all right. And he had walked into it like a dumb yearling! He seethed with helpless anger, directed at himself.

Passing through a second door, the gunman close behind him, Slade found himself in a dim corridor which ended in yet a third door leading to the outside, an alley lighted only by gleams from a street lamp at the corner. Three saddled and bridled horses stood patiently by the wall.

"Fork the one to the left," said the gunman. "Easy, now."

Slade did as he was bid. With swift skill, his ankles were lashed to the stirrup straps.

"Hands behind you," came an order. Another moment and his wrists were securely tied together with rawhide thongs. His captors mounted. One seized the bridle of Slade's horse and moved down the alley at a swift pace.

The alley opened onto a dark and deserted street. Five minutes later they were beyond the city's limits and riding north through the star-burned night. Slade broke the silence for the first time.

"Just what's the idea of this kidnapping?" he asked.

"You'll find out," the thickset man replied. "We know you, *El Halcon,* know you make a business of hornin' in on good things other folks have started, and getting away with it. Not this time, though. This time you're up against a smarter man than you are."

Slade did not argue the statement, for he grimly admitted there might well be an unpleasant element of truth in it.

"The boss wants to talk to you," his captor continued. "He first figured to kill you, then changed his mind and allowed maybe he could use you. Maybe you'll make out with him, I dunno. I figure what he has in mind is too big for any fooling around."

"You've been doing pretty well, haven't you?" Slade probed.

"Oh, so-so," the other answered. "Good spending money, but the boss says what he has in mind will make it look like chicken feed. Guess it will; he's a hombre with plenty of savvy."

Slade was inclined to agree that it was very likely so. He relapsed into silence again. There was no sense in continuing the conversation. All he could do was let events shape their course and watch for opportunity. He knew he was on a very hot spot, with scant chance of getting off it alive. In his opinion, the mysterious boss was after information of some kind and when he had learned or failed to learn what he was interested in, his prisoner would get short shrift.

Mile after mile they rode at a steady gait. Slade fervently hoped they were nearing the end of the journey, wherever the devil that might be, for his arms were aching intolerably and his wrists and ankles were raw and sore from the chafing of his bonds.

Finally, a dark shadow took form on the northern horizon and Slade knew they were approaching the Big Thicket. Another half-hour and they were riding slowly through the deep gloom beneath the great trees. Soon, however, birds began chirping and the darkness grayed. When the dawn broke he saw they were following a narrow track that wound between bristles of growth, boring deeper and deeper into the sinister depths of the Thicket.

For nearly two more hours they rode steadily and Slade's discomfort had increased to acute torture. His captors slumped wearily in their saddles, glancing at him occasionally from bloodshot eyes.

The thickset bearded man broke the silence he had maintained for hours.

"You can take it, all right," he said grudgingly. "Not much farther to go and we'll take those ropes off you. Guess you'll be more comfortable then — for a while."

A grin twisted the thin lips of the lanky man, a very evil grin, Slade thought.

"Uh-huh — for a while," he repeated. His companion glowered at him.

"You're too blasted fond of seeing fellers squirm and yell," he growled. "I don't mind killings, but torturin' folks ain't in my line. I'm hanged if I don't believe you've got Injun blood."

"I do what I'm told to do," the other replied, his voice a snarl. "If you don't like it, take it up with the boss. See what *he* tells *you.*"

The bearded man did not answer and Slade thought he winced a little at what Dirk's remark implied.

A little later, to Slade's infinite relief, they reached a small clearing in which stood a weatherbeaten cabin built of logs and roofed with split poles. Over to one side was a straggle of dwarfed corn and a few green globes of stunted melons. Doubtless the clearing had once been much larger, but the Big Thicket encroaches rapidly on cut-over lands and was reclaiming its own. Slade knew that scattered within its tangles were the cleared places of settlers who waged a constant fight against the rapid growth. Very likely the cabin had been built and occupied by one such who, long since, had either died or had acknowledged defeat and moved away.

There was a lean-to near the cabin, to which his captors led the way. The lashings were removed and he was allowed to dismount, so stiff and sore he could hardly move.

"Into the shack with you," Dirk growled and followed close behind as Slade stumbled forward on wooden legs. The other man remained behind to care for the horses.

With Dirk's gun muzzle prodding his back, Slade shoved open the door and found himself in a fairly large room that showed signs of recent extensive occupancy. Bunks were built against the walls. There was an ample store of staple provisions stacked on shelves, and a quantity of coarse crockery. Cooking utensils hung from pegs driven between the logs. A large stone fireplace was equipped with hooks for pots and kettles. Also a Dutch oven. A bucket of water stood on a low shelf. There was a table and half a dozen chairs. A number of rifles stood in a corner. Without doubt the place was an outlaw hangout, perhaps that of the sinister Twilight Riders.

A glance around was all that was vouchsafed him. Dirk was prodding him across the room to an open door. "In there," he ordered. Slade enered a smaller room lighted by a single barred window and the door was slammed behind him. He heard the snick of a shot bolt.

The room, while smaller than the one he had just left, was still of pretty good size but was devoid of furniture other than a bunk built against the far wall, on which was a heavy corn-shuck mattress and several dirty blankets.

Slade sat down on the bunk, massaging his numb wrists and ankles until the circulation became normal and he felt much better. In the outer room, he could hear Dirk grumbling about being tired and sleepy.

"Oh, shut up!" his companion snapped. "If you weren't all the time swiggin' red-eye you wouldn't be so sleepy. What you kicking about? You can tumble into bed and go to sleep, while I've got to ride back to town and meet the boss. But don't you open that door," he cautioned. "You've got a slippery customer on your hands and if you let him slide through your fingers, what the boss'll do to you will make your own hot irons and wirecutters look tame."

Dirk replied with a torrent of oaths. "Don't worry," he finished. "That door's stayin' shut and locked, and I'll sleep with one eye open."

"You'd better," grunted the other. "Well, so long. I'm moseying."

The outer door slammed and a moment later there was a tapping of hoofs on the grass of the clearing, fading away into the distance. Slade got up and silently approached the door, which was constructed of stout planks. There were cracks between the vertical planks, and placing his eye to one, he had a fairly good view of the outer room. The first thing to catch his gaze was his own guns lying on the table. They were only a few feet distant from where he stood, but they might as well be in Mexico for all the good they were likely to do him, he reflected morosely. He could see Dirk moving about, grumbling to himself. Finally he stretched out on one of the bunks and almost immediately began to snore. Slade proceeded to give his prison a careful once-over.

The results of his examination were not satisfactory. The walls were of heavy logs, firm and free from rot. The puncheon floor was solidly laid and pegged.

He tested the window bars and shook his head. They were firmly fixed in the logs, undoubtedly having been placed to discourage predatory animals that might attempt to break into what had probably been a storeroom. Slade returned to the bunk, sat down and rolled a cigarette.

Eight

Slade knew the situation was desperate. By nightfall, probably, or a little later, the boss, whoever the devil he was, would arrive at the cabin and very quickly it would be curtains. He gathered from what the bearded man said that the boss had a sadistic streak, and there was no doubt that Dirk had one. Slade had no intention of being tortured to death. When the door was opened, he would charge out fighting and force them to kill him. That was the grim alternative which confronted him. Not a pleasant prospect.

Pinching out the cigarette, he examined the door again, which appeared to be the only possible avenue of egress. The planks were thick and strong and securely bolted to the cross pieces. The hinges were on the outside, which eliminated any chance of loosening them. Only a battering ram would knock down the barrier, and he didn't have one, even if he could get it into operation quickly enough to smash the door before Dirk snapped out of it and grabbed his gun. Just the same, if he could only contrive something of the sort, he'd take a chance of escaping Dirk's bullet and snatching his own guns from the table. He went back to the bunk and examined it. It was nailed to the wall, but when he heaved on the outer edge the nails seemed to give a little. He stepped back and contemplated the thing. The frame which supported the mattress was stout and heavy. Another try and he was convinced that with something to use as a pry he could loosen it from the wall; but where was something that would serve as a pry?

Getting down on his hands and knees he peered beneath the bunk in hope that some loosened beam of wood might be there.

No beam was visible, only a chunky square box. Curious as to what it might contain, he hauled it out. Then he rocked back on his heels, staring. The box was more than half full of stubby, greasy cylinders. And now he saw that on its sides was ominous red lettering — *Dynamite!*

And lying a little to one side was a coil of fuse and a supply of detonating caps.

Fingering one of the sticks, he contemplated his find and its significance. Very likely the missing sticks had been used to blow derricks and it was reasonable to assume that the cabin was the hangout of whoever was waging war against the oil field, presumably the Twilight Riders.

Well, anyhow, he didn't have to worry about a death by torture. He could blow the cabin and its occupants to kingdom come on a moment's notice. Fortunate for him that his two captors had forgotten the box under the bunk and had neglected to remove it. He chuckled softly as he envisioned the consternation beyond the closed door when those in the outer room heard the sharp hissing of the burning fuse cut to almost instantly detonate the cap.

Suddenly his eyes glowed as they fixed on the stout wooden barrier. A stick of the stuff would smash that door to splinters. Of course there was more than an even chance that the concussion would explode the rest of the dynamite and blow the cabin and him to Louisiana, but it was worth taking that chance.

He studied the door. No need to use a whole stick. A third of one would be plenty and would lessen the risk of setting off the remainder of the box.

His captors had refrained from taking the

contents of his pockets. He drew his clasp knife and began to cut off a segment of the stick. It was a ticklish business and he set his teeth as the blade bit through the wax paper and grated on the nitroglycerine-impregnated mixture. Working with the greatest care, sawing slowly to minimize friction heat, he cut through the stick. The larger section he replaced in the box. The smaller he capped and fused with a short length of fuse. Then he wrapped the box in the blankets and shoved it as far under the bunk as it would go. The capped and fused section he placed against the bottom of the door, wedging it in place, careful not to make the slightest sound. Picking up the heavy husk mattress from the bunk slats, he placed it over the stick to minimize the outward blow of the concussion.

The sputter of the burning fuse might arouse Dirk, but it was reasonable to believe that he would at once make for the door to see what was going on, which would certainly eliminate him as a hazard.

Setting his eye to a crack between the planks, Slade studied the outer room. The bunk on which Dirk lay was directly across from the door. He believed that if the dynamite reacted properly and smashed the door, he should be able to reach the bunk before Dirk could get into action. He earnestly desired to take the fellow alive if possible. For despite his apparent ferocious cruelty, he figured Dirk to be a weakling who could be induced to talk, reveal the identity of the mysterious boss and give information that would enable him to smash the outlaw gang.

First, however, he had to escape alive from his prison and he estimated the chances of doing so unscathed were about fifty-fifty.

"Well, here we go," he muttered, "maybe for a quick trip to eternity."

He struck a match and touched it to the dangerously short fuse. With the first sputtering rain of sparks he leaped erect, sped across the room and crouched facing the far corner, protecting the back of his head with his hands. Belatedly he realized he would have done much better to throw the percussion caps through the window bars.

Short though it was, the fuse took what seemed to be an eternity to burn to the cap. Then the muffled boom, the hammer blows of displaced air and Slade was knocked off his feet. The mattress, its grease-soaked cover burning fiercely, was hurled clear across the room to land on the bunk, raining sparks on the blanket-swathed box of dynamite. Where the door had been was a gaping hole swirling with acrid fumes and yellow smoke. Slade bounded through the opening and caught a glimpse of Dirk rising wild-eyed from his bunk. He surged erect as Slade closed with him. Instantly they were locked in a deadly grapple, while the draught pouring through the shattered windows sent the flames in the other room roaring to the roof.

Slade had pinned Dirk's gunhand to his side and sought to get a grip on the outlaw's throat. But Dirk, though lean and lanky, was broad of shoulder, deep of chest. He seemed to be made of steel wires and was supple as a snake. Dashing Slade's clutching hand aside, he sent a crashing blow against his jaw that flashed red streaks before the ranger's eyes and almost caused him to lose his grip on Dirk's wrist. His countering blow was blocked. Dirk caught him on the chin with his elbow, snapping his head back, then took one himself that smashed his nose and spurted blood from his lips.

Back and forth they writhed and lurched, overturned chairs going to matchwood under their feet, thudding into the wall, caroming off the bunks. Slade fought frantically, for at any moment the fire in the other room would heat the caps until they exploded and in turn set off the dynamite. If that happened, neither of them had a chance in the world to escape alive. Dirk frothed curses through his bloody lips, but Slade fought in grim silence.

Slade stepped on the rung of a shattered chair. It rolled under his foot, threw him off balance. With a yell of triumph, Dirk tore free and went for his gun. Slade made a desperate grab for his own Colts on the table, and got them. Dirk fired. The slug ripped a stinging furrow in Slade's thigh and hurled him sideways with a shock. Dirk's second bullet grained his upper arm. Back and forth through the swirling smoke and the dynamite fumes gushed the orange flashes, the reports slamming against the roar of the flames. It was almost blind shooting, so thick was the smoke. Slade was firing with both hands as fast as he could pull trigger, while his ears strained for the thunder of doom in the inner room.

Suddenly Dirk screamed, a strange and bubbling scream that snapped off short. His body thudded to the floor, blood gushing from his bullet-slashed throat. Slade leaped over the body, flung the door open and fled the cabin. Swerving, he raced to the lean-to, where the two terrified horses were snorting and plunging and striving to break loose.

There was no time to get a rig on one or to untie the halter knots. Slade whipped out his knife and slashed the ropes. With a bound he forked one animal, jerked its head around by the rope and sent it speeding for the growth, the other clattering beside its fellow.

They had just reached the edge of the clearing when the dynamite let go with a crash that seemed to shake the heavens, nearly knocking the horses off their feet. A blinding yellowish flash dimmed the sunlight, followed by clouds of smoke and the thudding of blazing timbers on the ground.

Deafened, his eyes dazzled, his head ringing like a bell, Slade clung to the mane of his mount. The demoralized animal needed no urging to go away from there. Through the growth it tore, regardless of thorns and minor obstacles, swerving around trees, leaping over fallen trunks. It had covered a full half-mile before Slade was able to bring it under control to stand with heaving sides and hanging head, utterly spent. Its companion, which had carried no load, was in little better case.

Slade dismounted, sat down with his back against a tree and rolled a cigarette with fingers that shook from strain and fatigue. His jaw was sore, the slight flesh wound in his thigh pained and his head felt like a stepped-on accordion. But he was darned glad to be able to feel at all, which for a time appeared far from hopeful.

"Well, critters," he told the horses, "the Twilight Riders, or somebody, are going to need a new hole-up. Blazes, what a blast! I thought the sky was going to cave in. Dirk sent word to wherever he went that he was on his way. I'm getting just a mite weary of dynamite, although it served me well, no doubt as to that. And now where in blazes are we? You got any notion?"

If the horses knew, they wouldn't admit it. Slade's eyes grew thoughtful as he noted that each bore Dunlap Jefferson's Diamond brand.

"That catty-cornered burn is getting to be a little monotonous," he observed. "Too much so to make good sense."

For some minutes he studied the brands, the concentration furrow deepening between his black brows, a sign that *El Halcon* was doing some thinking.

"A funny one, this," he mused aloud. "Yes, almighty funny. Don't often see a burn run that way anymore. I've a notion this requires a little looking into."

112

He pinched out the cigarette and examined his bullet-furrowed thigh, deciding that the wound was of little consequence.

"But it sure left a gap in my Levi's," he grumbled. "Big enough to let plenty of wind through. Well, feller, suppose we try and find water. I think we could all three use some about now."

Rising, he removed the halter from one animal and with the two bits of rope contrived a crude but workable bridle. Then he mounted and rode on, the second horse ambling along behind.

Before long they reached a small stream, the banks of which were clothed in grass. All three had a hearty drink. The horses began cropping. Slade sat down and smoked another cigarette. The sun was directly overhead and no good as a guide, but Slade knew that here the winds were prevailingly from the south and had left their mark on isolated trees, so he had no trouble getting his bearings. And if he followed a westerly course he must eventually reach the open prairie.

However, following a westerly course, or any other definite course, proved no easy task because of the Big Thicket's wild tangle of growth. The ground was a network of game tracks which apparently started from nowhere and led to the same place. As the afternoon wore on and the shadows lengthened, Slade was forced to admit that he was hopelessly lost.

Also, he was very weary after a sleepless night, and riding bareback didn't help.

Tired as he was, he had to chuckle at the thought of the bewilderment of the boss and his men when they arrived at where the cabin had stood and found only a hole in the ground. To watch their faces would be as good as a play, and their remarks would be something worth listening to. Very likely they would conclude that he had been killed by the explosion and when a "ghost" rode into town they would get something of a start, if they happened to be there at the time.

That is, he concluded morosely, if he didn't keep wandering around in this exaggerated cactus patch till he starved to death.

It was beginning to look as if he was due to do just that when to his great relief, as the shadows of twilight were curdling in the deeper hollows, the track he was following led him to a clearing similar to, but much larger than the one in which the outlaw cabin had stood. This was cultivated and fine crops of corn, beans, melons and other vegetables grew on the rich soil.

At the far end of the clearing stood a cabin, weathered by age but in an excellent state of repair. Blooming vines trailed over the logs and there were flowerbeds under the two windows. Evidently the cabin was occupied and not by transients.

As he neared the building, Slade let out a shout, for it was wise to announce one's self before riding up to a lonely cabin in the Big Thicket when night was close at hand. A moment later the door opened and a colored man appeared. He was evidently very old for his face was a network of wrinkles and his woolly thatch was snow white. But he was lance-straight and his brown eyes were bright and youthful, with a twinkle of humor in their depths.

The twinkle become more pronounced as they looked Slade over from head to foot.

"Boss, you sure must have been in some bobberty," he said, his voice rich and chuckley. "And I bet the other feller is worth looking at," he added, measuring Slade's tall form with his glance, the chuckle coming to the fore.

"I've a notion he is, if you could find him," Slade replied soberly.

The old man looked perplexed. "Just what do you all mean by that, boss?" he asked.

Honesty and truth were written plainly on

the wrinkled face and Slade proceeded to tell him exactly what happened, beginning with the kidnapping in the sheriff's office.

The Negro listened intently and shook his white head when Slade paused.

"Man, oh, man!" he said. "You all sure must have mixed up with the Twilight Riders. Mighty bad men, those Twilight Riders."

Slade agreed, without reservation.

"And you blowed up their cabin?" the other continued. "That was a good chore, but they'll find another one. Lots of old cabins around the Thicket. Folks build 'em, stay a while and then leave. Mighty lonesome in the Thicket, for some folks."

"Looks like you've been here quite a while," Slade commented, glancing around.

"Yes, boss, I have," the old man answered. "Man and boy, I've lived here in the Thicket for better'n forty years."

"And you don't get lonesome?" Slade asked. The old man smiled with a flash of white teeth and shook his head.

"No, boss, I don't get lonesome," he replied. "I got the birds and the little critters, and the wind in the trees at night for company, and the crick over there to talk to me and shine bright when the sun is shining. No, I don't never get lonesome. I try to think good thoughts, and good thoughts are mighty fine company."

Slade smiled down at him from his great height, and abruptly his cold eyes were all kindness.

"And make for happiness and contentment," he said. "I guess nobody is ever really lonesome who has good thoughts for company."

The old man smiled in turn. "And, boss, I got a notion you ain't ever over-lonesome," he replied.

"Thank you," Slade said simply.

"But light off, boss, light off," the other said. "Soon be gettin' dark. We'll put the beasts o' burden in the stable 'longside my mule and look after them. Then, there's cornpone in the oven and stewed chicken in the pot, and if you don't mind settin' at table with me —"

"I will be honored," Slade interrupted. "And thank you. I haven't eaten for so long my stomach's beginning to think my throat's been cut."

The oldster chuckled. "Then get ready to bust your buttons," he said. "My name's Prescott, Eben Prescott, mostly knowed as Uncle Eben."

Slade supplied his own name and held out his hand as he dismounted, which the old man took diffidently.

"You say those horses belonged to the outlaw fellers?" he remarked. "See they're wearing Mr. Dunlap Jefferson's Diamond."

"Yes," Slade agreed. "Uncle Eben, do you notice anything peculiar about those burns?"

The old man inspected them closely. "Uh-huh," he said. "They ain't been burned with a stampin' iron. Those Diamonds were run with a slick-iron. Mighty good work, too."

"Yes," Slade agreed again, "mighty good work. Needs a close look to tell they were run with a smooth, straight rod and not with a made-to-order branding iron that burns the brand on the hide with one quick stamp."

Uncle Eben nodded his understanding and they led the animals to the stable where they were stalled beside a pensive-looking mule named Susie, Uncle Eben informed Slade. Then they repaired to the cosily-furnished cabin which boasted chairs, a table, two bunks built against the walls, and cooking facilities.

"You said you got nicked in the leg, didn't you?" asked Uncle Eben. "I'm going to have a look at that nick."

"Nothing but a scratch," Slade deprecated the wound.

"Maybe," conceded Uncle Eben, "but in the Thicket you learn not to leave scratches to get well by themselves. Sometimes flies and other flyin' varmints lay eggs in 'em, and you have trouble. Uh-huh, that's quite a scratch. I got some stuff that's good for 'scratches' like this one. Real yarb medicine."

He proceeded to dress the ragged furrow with a mixture taken from a fruit jar.

"Feels soothing," Slade admitted.

"Uh-huh, it's that," said Uncle Eben, "and it'll keep you from getting a misery in that leg. There! Now we'll wash up and eat. Chicken and dumplin's look prime."

Slade decided that they were and proceeded to "bust his buttons," as Uncle Eben put it.

After eating, Slade rolled a cigarette. Uncle Eben hauled out an old black pipe and stuffed it with blacker tobacco.

"Some I growed in my own patch," he observed. "Mighty pow'ful, but got a good taste."

Content, they smoked in silence. They cleaned up the dishes together, Slade insisting on helping despite Uncle Eben's protests. By which time he was so sleepy he could hardly hold his eyes open. It was with a thankful heart that he turned to the comfortable bunk with its scrupulously clean blankets. Uncle Eben knelt beside his bed for a moment, his eyes closed, his hands clasped before him. Slade bowed his own black head during the prayer, and felt the better for it.

"Just a little habit of mine," Uncle Eben said as he stretched out. "I asks the Good Lawd to sort of look after the lots of folks what don't have it so easy and good like I do."

"And I've a notion He sort of looks after you, too," Slade smiled.

"Yes, I 'spects He does," replied the old man. "I'm way past seventy, and I ain't never been sick and I'm well and strong. Uh-huh, I guess He does."

After which they both went to sleep, and slept the sleep that comes to those whose hearts are clean.

NINE

When Slade awoke, sunshine was streaming gold through the windows and birds were singing in the thickets. Uncle Eben was already up and about, preparing breakfast. He smiled at Slade.

"Feeling better, eh?" he remarked. "The swole's going down in your face and you look plumb rested."

"I'm fine, thanks to you," Slade replied, springing lightly to his feet. "I think I'll go over to the creek and have a swim."

"Nice pool over there just past the clearing, I dug it out myself," said Uncle Eben. "No 'gators and no moccasins. Plenty of both in the bayous and the ponds, big ones."

Refreshed and invigorated by his dip in the cool water, Slade returned to the cabin, his black hair shining with moisture. Uncle Eben already had griddle cakes and bacon and eggs on the table, and mugs of steaming coffee. All of which Slade partook of hugely.

"Guess you'll be riding to town, now," observed his host. "I got a extra saddle you can use. Quite a ways to town. I'll show you how to get out of the Thicket. But you want to take care for those Twilight Riders — they're bad, and they'll be looking for you."

"I'll take care," Slade promised grimly.

Uncle Eben regarded him for a moment. "But don't forget, brother, that the Good Lawd said, 'Vengeance is mine, I'll do the repayin'.' "

"Yes," Slade agreed soberly, "but I think sometimes He needs an instrument to help Him repay."

Uncle Eben nodded his white head. "That's so," he said, adding, "Maybe I can lend a helpin' hand sometime."

"Yes, I think you can," Slade answered thoughtfully. "I think you can. Guess you know the Big Thicket pretty well."

"Reckon I know the Thicket as well as any man alive," replied Uncle Eben. "I know all the trails and where they go, even the ones to places where don't hardly anybody ever go, some of them mighty bad places. Think you'll know how to get back to my place here?"

"I can always get back to a place once I've

followed the road," Slade said confidently. "I'll be back soon with the rig you're lending me."

"Take your time, take your time," said Uncle Eben. "Be mighty glad to see you any time. You're real Buckra."

Slade bowed his head to the compliment, knowing that "Buckra" was the colored man's definition of a white man of high quality.

Shortly afterward they got the rigs on the horse Slade chose to ride, and the mule Susie.

"We'll take the other horse along with us and turn it loose on the prairie to fend for itself till somebody picks it up, which it can easily do," he decided. "I prefer not to leave it on your place. Some of those hellions might just possibly ride this way and spot it, which could mean trouble for you."

"Could be," agreed Uncle Eben. "I got no use for it anyhow; like my mule better. Riding Susie, I can just go to sleep if I'm tired and she'll get me home."

After a little more than an hour of riding, following a dim track that flowed steadily westward, they reached the open prairie a few miles north of the southern fringe of the Thicket. Here, Slade turned loose the led horse and shook hands with Uncle Eben.

"Thank you for everything," he said. "I'll be seeing you soon."

"Brother, you'll always be welcome," said the old man. "Hope you make it soon. And I'll be ready with a helping hand whenever you need me."

It was early afternoon when Slade approached Beaumont. Upon reaching town he headed straight for the stable where he kept Shadow. He turned the Diamond brand horse over to the stablekeeper.

"Keep him here till I call for him," he directed. "Don't let anyone other than myself take him out of here. Do you understand?"

The keeper, with Slade's eyes hard on his face, understood.

Next, Slade visited the sheriff's office. He found Sheriff Colton there with a bandaged head and a pain in his temper.

"So!" he greeted. "So you came back, eh?"

"Yes, I came back, although for a time I was rather doubtful about doing so," Slade answered. "What happened to you?"

"Your guess is as good as mine," the sheriff replied. "All I know is that night before last somebody called me to the door and when I stepped out onto the porch, the roof fell on me. Next thing I knew, when I woke up, I was sitting spraddled out in my chair with one heck of a headache. Dunlap Jefferson was in yesterday and wondered if it was you who walloped me one and rode off. Didn't make sense to me, though, and I told him so. Where you been?"

Slade told him. The sheriff swore until the air was blue. "If that ain't the limit!" he concluded. "You must have tangled with the Twilight Riders up at the Thicket the day you rode in here, and they were out to even the score."

"Looks sort of that way," Slade conceded. "I'd say they don't exactly hanker for interference."

The sheriff swore some more. Abruptly he fell silent, his eyes hard on Slade's face.

"Slade," he said, "I'm going to ask you a straight question, and I expect a straight answer."

"Shoot!" Slade replied composedly, a glint of amusement in his eyes. He knew perfectly well what was coming.

The sheriff hesitated, then spoke. "Slade," he said, "are you *El Halcon*?"

"Been called that," Slade answered, unperturbed.

"And what the devil are you doing here?"

Sheriff Colton demanded in exasperated tones.

"You'll find out, later," Slade replied.

"Yes, I don't doubt but I will," Colton said sarcastically. "From what I've heard of your reputation, I'm sure I will, and I'm liable to not like the finding."

"Might fool you," Slade said. "By the way, would you mind walking over to the stable where I keep my horse?"

"Why, no," the sheriff acceded, looking a trifle bewildered. "Going to get your critter and ride off?" he added hopefully.

"Later, but not today," Slade replied, smiling.

"I was afraid of that," the sheriff admitted. "I'm sort of beholden to you, Slade. If it wasn't for you, I've a notion about now I'd be pushing up the daisies. But just the same, you squattin' in a section means trouble."

"For some folks, I hope," Slade conceded. "If you feel up to the walk, let's go."

At the stable, Colton stared at the horse Slade had brought in and swore even more pungently than before.

"Another blasted Diamond!" he finished. "What in the heck!"

"Look close at the burn," Slade suggested. "See if you can note anything out of the ordinary about it."

Colton peered, traced the mark on the horse's hide with a tentative forefinger. "Darned if I don't believe it was made with a running iron, not a stamp," he said, a puzzled expression on his face.

"It was," Slade said. "Do the Diamond hands use slick-irons?"

"Why, no, I'd say," the sheriff replied hesitantly. "Of course I can't say for sure that some of the older hands don't. But I'm sure most of their work is done with a stamp."

"Most owners discourage the use of a slick-iron," Slade commented. "It's a waste of time and inflicts needless pain on the animal. In fact, as you must know, there's a Texas law against its usage, passed back in the seventies. It's purpose, of course, was to discourage rustling and brand blotters. After the law was passed it became the custom to use branding irons of a fixed stamp or pattern. But sometimes the law is disregarded by owners whose oldtimers like the running iron, although they don't ride around loose packing one."

"That's right," the sheriff agreed. "Then what does the burn on this critter's hide mean?"

"Suppose," Slade said, "that in the course

of a derrick being blown with dynamite, or a well set on fire, or a stage robbed, you got a look at the horses ridden by the outlaws and saw they were bearing a Diamond brand, what would you think?"

The answer was obvious, and the sheriff did not hedge. "I'd think," he replied, "that it looked sort of bad for the Diamond outfit."

"Which could have been the intention," Slade said.

"You mean to throw suspicion on the Diamond outfit?"

"Exactly. But that conclusion doesn't clear the Diamond outfit."

"How's that?"

"There's an angle to consider," Slade explained. "An angle that would very likely occur to a smart prosecutor. That the Diamond outfit ran the brands to confuse the issue."

"Confuse the issue?"

"Yes, so that if a horse happened to fall into the hands of law officers, say, they could point out that the brand was run by the outlaws for the purpose of throwing suspicion on their outfit. See?"

"Yes, I see," the sheriff said slowly. "Slade," he said wearily, "I wish I'd never laid eyes on you. You get me more mixed up by the minute. I don't know which end I'm standing on!"

"You'll end right side up," Slade predicted with a chuckle. "By the way, who told you I was *El Halcon*?"

"Dunlap Jefferson," the sheriff answered. "He said he saw you once over at Corpus Christi, and didn't forget you. Guess nobody would that ever saw you."

"Perhaps not," Slade conceded. "Especially if they happened to have good reason to remember me," he added cryptically.

Sheriff Colton shot him a quick look, but Slade did not elaborate.

"What else did Jefferson have to say about me?" he asked.

"Oh, no more than a lot of folks say, that you're an owlhoot too smart to get caught, and that your gun is for hire."

"Remember, *he* offered me a job," Slade smiled.

"That's right, so he did," the sheriff conceded, with a chuckle. "Only I don't remember anything being said about guns."

"A hand is naturally expected to fight for his employer," Slade pointed out.

"Now you're poking fun at me," snorted the sheriff. "Come on, let's go get a drink and something to eat. Sullivan's place all right?"

"Okay by me," Slade said. "Let's go."

As they walked toward the saloon, the sheriff remarked,

"Reckon there's no sense in figuring to hold an inquest on that jigger you downed at the cabin."

"Guess not," Slade agreed. "Doubt if there's enough of him left to sit on, even if I could locate the place, which is improbable. I got to thinking that perhaps I missed a bet by not trying to work my way back to that clearing and hanging around till the boss showed up. Might have been able to get a look at him. But I wasn't in very good shape and the notion didn't occur to me till I'd been wandering around through the brush for quite a while and then it was highly unlikely that I could have worked my way back."

"To try it with only a bareback nag and a halter for a bridle would have been plumb loco," grunted the sheriff.

"So I figured," Slade said, "but I sure would have liked to get a look at the sidewinder."

"You're liable to get the chance if you don't watch your step," warned the sheriff. "I'd say he's a hombre with plenty of moss on his horns, whoever the devil he is."

The sheriff wore a worried look as he

made the last remark. At that moment they reached Sullivan's and the conversation ceased.

However, while they were waiting for their order to be filled, the sheriff brought up the topic again, obliquely.

"Yes, a bunch with plenty of savvy," he remarked. "The way they set that trap for you was smart, mighty smart. Nothing bungley like waiting around a corner for you, when you'd naturally be on the watch."

"They didn't miss a detail," Slade said. "Even to propping you up in your chair so I'd see you through the window. I was caught completely offguard."

"Small blame to you," grunted Colton. "Who wouldn't have been?"

"A snake-blooded outfit, too," Slade resumed. "Taking a chance on killing a peace officer to further their plans. Hitting a man over the head with a gun barrel is risky business."

"You're darn right," agreed the sheriff, feeling gingerly of his bandaged skull.

"And," Slade added thoughtfully, "the way the affair was handled indicates a thorough knowledge of your habits and reactions, figuring that you'd step out onto the porch when somebody called you, and that you'd

131

likely be in your office at that particular time."

The sheriff nodded agreement. "I usually do my book work about that time," he commented. Again the worried look passed across his face. Slade noted it, and smiled. He knew very well that Colton was thinking of Dunlap Jefferson, which was what he desired, at the moment. The food arrived and was consumed mostly in silence. After his third cup of coffee, the sheriff attained a better humor.

"Reckon I should be happy, with outlaws fighting it out and cashing each other in, but I ain't," he said lugubriously. "One heck of a peace officer I've turned out to be! Here I am hobnobbin' with a feller who's said to be the slickest owlhoot in Texas!"

Suddenly his wrinkled old face broke into a grin that made it appear wonderfully youthful and pleasing.

"But, blast it! I like it."

Slade regarded him with dancing eyes. "To such base ends do we come," he smiled.

The sheriff chuckled, but was immediately serious again.

"And do you figure those hellions will find another hangout in the Thicket?" he asked.

"That's my opinion," Slade replied. "They'll need a base of operations, and from what Uncle Eben said, there are plenty of places they can use, and they evidently know the Thicket. Yes, I think they'll very quickly prepare another hole-up. At least I hope so. Then I'll at least know the general locality in which they should be found."

"And you figure to look for them?" the sheriff asked curiously.

"I do," Slade said.

"Got a sort of personal feud with them, eh?"

"By planning to kill me, after first torturing me, they made it, to a certain extent, personal," Slade replied. The sheriff nodded.

"I can understand that," he said, "but taking the law in your own hands is a risky business. One slip and you're in trouble."

"I'll try not to make a slip," Slade said, with a smile.

Sheriff Colton shook his head dubiously. "Well, I've got to be getting back to the office," he said, and glanced toward the door. "Here comes Jim Hogg, and that's Gates and Roche with him, isn't it?"

"That's right," Slade replied.

The three magnates glanced about, spotted the table and came hurrying across the room. The warmth with which they greeted Slade was not lost on the sheriff. Jim Hogg looked decidedly relieved.

"So here you are!" he exclaimed. "I was afraid maybe — maybe you decided to leave the section."

"Not just yet," Slade smiled, "although I came pretty close to it. Do you know Sheriff Colton?"

"I've heard of him, of course, but I never had the pleasure of meeting him personally," Hogg said, extending his hand. "How are you, Sheriff?"

"I'm a mixed-up man," sighed the peace officer.

"Guess we all are! Guess we all are!" said Gates as he shook hands. "If there ever came a time when I wasn't mixed-up in one way or another, I wouldn't know myself. Have a drink with us before you go."

Sheriff Colton nodded acceptance and sat down again.

"I hope you'll keep this young rapscallion out of trouble," Hogg said, with a glance at Slade.

"I'll try," the sheriff promised, "but I'm scairt it'll be considerable of a chore. Trouble just nacherly follows him around."

"Without trouble there would be no progress," Roche said sententiously. "All progress involves the upsetting of existent ideas, and that almost invariably causes trouble."

The sheriff looked puzzled, but Slade nodded sober agreement.

"How is your friend Rader?" he asked Gates. The Wall Street man snorted.

"That fellow has me puzzled," he complained. "As I mentioned the other night, I was quite interested in his movements. I had two of my best men all set to follow him and try and learn whom he contacted, but he never showed up for the train. Didn't show up for the next one, either, and that was all for the day. Haven't seen hide nor hair of him since the poker game the other night. He's a smooth one."

"Yes, I've a notion he is," Slade agreed, his eyes thoughtful.

After a couple of drinks, the sheriff left for his office. Gates and Roche also took their departure, having a business appointment. Slade and Hogg were left alone at the table. "All right," said the latter, "let's have it. What happened? I know darn well something did."

Slade told him, in detail. The former governor outdid the sheriff's finest efforts at swearing.

"That's the limit!" he exploded. "Slade,

have you any notion who runs that infernal outfit?"

"I'm beginning to get one, but so far I haven't much to go on, and I could be wrong, so I'm not naming any names just yet," Slade replied.

"I'll wager that when you come up with the answer it will be something of a shock to the section," Hogg predicted.

"To a portion of it, perhaps, if I'm not making a mistake," Slade said.

"You're not given to making mistakes," Hogg grunted. "Well, I know there's no use trying to get anything out of you till you're ready to talk, but I'm darned curious."

"Be careful," Slade smiled, "remember, curiosity was fatal to a certain domestic animal."

"Uh-huh, but satisfaction brought it back to life again," the ex-governor misquoted. "Well, now what? Going to stick around town for a while?"

"I think tomorrow I may ride to the Diamond spread to have a little talk with Dunlap Jefferson," Slade replied.

"A fine idea," Hogg applauded heartily. "Take some handcuffs along."

Slade smiled, but did not comment.

"I've got to be moving along," said the

magnate. "Suppose you'll be at the hotel later?"

"I expect to be," Slade said.

"Okay," Hogg nodded. "Perhaps I'll see you there. Keep me informed if anything breaks."

"I will," Slade promised.

Ten

Slade sat on at the table for a little while, smoking and thinking; but as it was still early, presently he left the saloon for a walk around the town, which he found increasingly interesting.

Even more so were the discussions that raged in various places, which caused his brows to knit.

"I tell you the oil people are about fed up," a portly merchant was declaring to a group of companions at a bar. "Firing that well the other night has wore their patience mighty thin. A little more and a bunch that'll know how to shoot will ride over to Dunlap Jefferson's place and clean house. You watch and see!"

"No proof that Jefferson had anything to do with firing that well," protested another shopkeeper.

"No, there's no proof," conceded the first speaker, "but as the old sayin' goes, where there's a lot of smoke there's mighty apt to be some fire. Jefferson has been sounding off big about the oil folks, and he's chased drillers off state land, threatening to shoot them if they come back. And he talked the cowmen hereabouts into not selling beef to the oil people, so that they have to have it shipped in from Port Arthur. You're going to have trouble making the oil people believe Jefferson didn't have a hand in blowing the derricks and firing the well. I tell you it's going to end up just like it did when the rice growers barged in, years back."

"Rice growers and the cowmen get along all right now," somebody observed.

"Uh-huh, but there was quite a few shootings before they settled down peaceful together. This time it'll be worse."

"I don't like it," another speaker complained. "It's bad for business. That is, except for them what deal in powder and lead."

This brought a chuckle, but the group was immediately serious again. Slade could see that they were really worried, and not without cause. He resolved that he certainly would take a ride to the Diamond ranch next day.

It was dark when Slade returned to Sullivan's place. He sat down at a table near the wall, where it was rather shadowy, and from which he had a good view of the room, and ordered coffee. What he had overheard while walking about town was disturbing and gave him much food for thought.

He had just finished a second cup and was wondering what would be good to eat when Berne Rader entered. He was dusty and travel-stained in a manner that was never attained on a railroad train. Slade concluded that Rader had been doing some long and hard riding. He regarded the speculator with interest.

Rader walked to the bar and ordered a drink, which he downed at a gulp and immediately ordered another, which he drank more slowly. Slade instinctively glanced toward the big table in the corner. Yes, a game was getting underway there. He saw Rader also glance in that direction.

However, the speculator did not immediately repair to the game. He ordered still a third drink and as he sipped it, a man in range clothes approached him and said a few words. Rader started visibly, and Slade saw an incredulous expression cross his face. He turned to the man and apparently asked a question. The other spoke at length, and Rader shook his head as in bewilderment. He gestured to the bartender to fill the glasses, and asked another question or two, to which his companion replied briefly, tossed off his drink and sauntered away. Rader remained at the bar, brooding over his glass, shaking his head from time to time as one who is perplexed. Finally he swallowed his fourth drink, turned and repaired to the poker game. After a word or two with the players, he drew up a chair and sat down. Slade lighted a cigarette and ordered a meal.

Slade's gaze had followed the man who had spoken to Rader and was now idling at the far end of the bar. He was a lean, sinewy individual with a tight mouth and cold, watchful eyes very light in color. He looked to be a hard man and quite likely was. Slade studied him and concluded that he was, or had been, a cowhand. A gun worn on his left side, butt to the front, indicated the cross-pull man. Slade thought probably he was a master of that difficult but very fast draw. Altogether, not exactly what would be expected of an associate of the speculator. The brief conversation between the two had been predicated, Slade thought, upon more than a casual acquaintanceship. Whatever it was he told Rader had disturbed the recipient of the information not a little; Rader had evinced something close to consternation, and had appeared reluctant to accept what the other had advanced as authentic. Well, any form of gambling sometimes made strange bed-fellows.

While occupied with his food, Slade found time to note all that was going on around him. Everything was quiet enough for the moment. Berne Rader's whole attention appeared centered on his cards. His face was flushed, his eyes glowing. Evidently he was gripped by the gambling fever to the exclusion of all else.

An argument started at the bar. Near the man who had spoken to Rader were several oil workers in greasy overalls and spotted shirts. They were drinking heavily and one in particular, a big rigger, was growing belligerent. He spoke to the man, who paid no attention to him, raised his voice and spoke again, and again he was ignored. He let out a bellow about "blasted cowhands," took a step forward, huge fist raised as if to strike.

The man moved. His right hand whipped across his waist and the big gun fairly leaped from its sheath. But there was no crash of a report, just a slashing backhand stroke, the crunch of the heavy steel barrel against bone, and the rigger was sprawled senseless on the floor, blood pouring from his split scalp. The man, the gun still in his hand, glanced questioningly at the rigger's companions. They showed no disposition to take up the quarrel. The gun flipped back in its holster. The man raised his glass and took a drink.

Yes, a hard man!

Slade glanced toward the corner. The poker table was apparently oblivious to what had happened at the bar. In fact, the whole affair had been settled with such dispatch that hardly anybody took note of it. A few people at nearby tables rose to their feet, and sat down again.

Two swampers, with Terry Sullivan looming behind, carried the rigger to the back room to get patched up. When he regained consciousness, he would be ushered out the back door and told to scoot. Slade ordered another cup of coffee.

The man finished his drink and without a glance at the subdued oil workers, sauntered out. Slade waited around for quite a while, but he did not return. Berne Rader was fully occupied with his poker game. Slade did not believe that the speculator had noticed him, sitting against the wall in the shadow as he was. A little later he headed for the Crosby House and bed.

Slade arose early the following morning.

There were very few people in the Crosby House dining room at that hour and he enjoyed a quiet and leisurely breakfast. After eating, he rolled a cigarette and reviewed recent events, endeavoring to weave them into a definite pattern with the help of scraps of information he had gleaned from his conversations with Jim Hogg and Bet-a-Million Gates. The result of his cogitations was a change of his plans for the day. He pinched out his cigarette, repaired to the livery stable and got the rig on Shadow.

However, he did not ride west by north to Dunlap Jefferson's holding; his visit to the Diamond ranchhouse could wait. He turned Shadow's nose south by slightly east.

The reason for his change of plan was an apparently insignificant thing. Nothing more than the gray dust on Berne Rader's clothes. Dust that could not have been acquired on a railroad train but which could easily have accumulated in the course of a long horseback ride, just such a ride as Slade now had before him, the twenty-mile ride to Port Arthur on Sabine Lake.

John Warne Gates was confident that Rader did not take a train to Port Arthur; but the railroad was not the only means of transportation available to the promoter. Rader's remark about catching a train may have been for the purpose of throwing Gates off the track. As a result, Gates' men watched the railroad while Rader proceeded blithely to Port Arthur via horseback.

Gates had also appeared convinced that Rader was in some way connected with one of the big syndicates vieing for power and profit in this section of Texas.

Slade knew that the struggle between the great interests had been, and was, prolonged and bitter, with no holds barred. From that struggle might well have developed the situation which was causing so much trouble in the section.

He hardly believed that the two syndicates were really mixed up in the business, but he could not afford to pass up any leads. Especially when he had no definite suspect with the possible exception of Dunlap Jefferson. And as to Jefferson he was dubious, although he knew he could be wrong. Well, he might learn something in Port Arthur. There was a man in the lake city who would very likely be able to impart information that might help. It did seem a bit ridiculous that the syndicates composed of nationally prominent businessmen should be subject to suspicion, but sometimes underlings got out of hand. The bloody cattle and land wars of the West attested to that. And when great interests were battling for control, strange things sometimes happened.

Slade knew that the row between the rival interests began with the founding of Port Arthur and had continued through the years. Port Arthur, unlike most Texas communities, didn't just grow; it was planned and built.

The development of Port Arthur became the dream, ultimately realized, by Arthur Stilwell, a promoter and a member of a wealthy pioneering New York family. He was the builder of the Kansas City, Pittsburgh & Gulf Railroad and the head of a million-dollar organization at the age of twenty-eight.

Stilwell believed in hunches and also believed, or pretended to believe, in supernatural creatures he whimsically called "Brownies." He maintained that the Brownies had urged him to choose the Port Arthur site when he was looking around for a Gulf terminus for his railroad. More likely he was swayed by a shrewd evaluation of natural advantages and the coming development of the region. Anyhow he claimed that he was able, in his dreams and with a little assistance by the Brownies, to envision Port Arthur, exact in all detail, as it was subsequently developed. He insisted that this city was the only one ever located and built under direction from the spirit world. Hard-headed financiers scoffed at this claim but were unanimous in admitting Stilwell's shrewdness and vision.

Stilwell also built a railroad from Port Arthur to Beaumont to freight supplies from Beaumont to the booming new town. The Kountz interests, that envisaged a development of the Sabine Pass and the Neches River into a dependable waterway, and Beaumont as a deep-water port, didn't favor the railroad, as they were later to look askance at the pipeline from the Beaumont oil fields to Port Arthur. That, however, didn't stop Stilwell. He built a ship canal and docks, neither pleasing to the Kountz interests, and proceeded to develop his town.

But, as is often the case with promoters, Stilwell spread himself a bit too thin. His labyrinthine enterprises needed more money. He turned to John Warne Gates, destined to be the second of Port Arthur's colorful promoters. Gates bought stock in Stilwell's companies, and soon, by shrewd manipulations, brought them under his control. Stilwell was convinced that he had been frozen out. Embittered and mad as a hornet, he flounced off to Europe vowing revenge.

So Gates, with his oil wells and railroad and other vast interests found the Kountz people, aided and abetted now by Stilwell, arrayed against him.

Such financial shenanigans were common enough among the money Titans of Wall Street and the East, where the contest was usually fought out with proxies and stock-holders' ballots; but Walt Slade knew that here in the still far from tame Border country, ballots might well be supplanted or supplemented by bullets. The code of ethics practiced by the big fellows didn't always trickle down to the lower echelons. And now and then gentlemen of easy conscience and "share-the-wealth" notions found such conditions remunerative when accompanied by side issues of their own, which sometimes entailed such minor matters as robbery and murder.

Slade considered that it was imperative for him to learn whether present conditions in the section were an offshoot of the current row between the syndicates. If so, by concentrating on Dunlap Jefferson and his ilk he might well be riding a cold trail.

From where he rode, Slade could catch an occasional glimpse of the railroad, and in the still farther distance, the wavering silver flash of the Neches River edging away to reach Sabine Lake. He watched a combination passenger and freight train crawling along like a discouraged worm, the locomotive's stack belching peevish clouds of undigested smoke; he could almost hear the fireman cursing the kind of coal he was forced to shovel into the protesting firebox, and the engineer's jovial comments to his perspiring assistant. He chuckled as he recalled the railroader's old saying, "A fireman is an individual with a weak head and a strong back; an engineer is a fireman whose back has also gotten weak." Firemen agreed wholeheartedly with the latter clause of the statement, and changed their minds when they were promoted to the right side of the cab.

ELEVEN

Slade reached Port Arthur around noon. He stabled his horse and sauntered along Stilwell Boulevard until he came to a plate glass window across which was legended,

Airley Gibbs
Attorney at Law

Pushing open the door, he entered. A very pretty receptionist, not too old and not too young, looked up from her desk.

"Can I do something for you, sir?" she asked in a gentle and pleasingly modulated voice.

"I'd like to see Mr. Gibbs," Slade replied.

The receptionist looked doubtful, casting a glance at a closed inner door.

"He is very busy —" she began hesitantly.

Slade was about to give his name, then refrained. He saw a chance for some amusement from the situation. So instead, he smiled, the little devils of laughter dancing in the back of his eyes.

The receptionist also smiled, and blushed prettily. "I'll speak to him," she said and passed through the inner door, leaving it slightly ajar. Slade heard the sweet voice say,

"Mr. Gibbs, there is a cowboy who wishes to see you."

There followed a roar like that of an annoyed sea lion: "A cowboy! What the blankety-blank-blank does a cowboy want to see me for? Tell him —"

"I really think you should see him, Mr. Gibbs," the gentle and composed voice interrupted.

"Who told you you could think?" bawled the sea lion. "I do the thinking around here! *I'll* see *him!*"

Feet pounded the floor with a ponderous rhythm, the door banged wide open and the sea lion himself stood framed in it. He was a wondrously fat man, more than six feet tall with shoulders in proportion and a barrel chest. His sleeves were rolled up to reveal corded, abnormally long arms like the stumped branches of an oak. He had a huge bald head, a rubicund face, a straggle of mustache. Hot little blue eyes set deep in rolls of flesh completed the resemblance.

He glared at his visitor and his bellow shook the rafters.

"Slade!"

He rushed forward, astonishingly light on his feet for such a big man, and wrapped the oak-stump arms about the ranger, fairly lifting him off his feet, and pounding his back with blacksmith's blows.

"You're pretty blasted big, but old Airley can handle you," he declared to the accompaniment of shivering window panes. "Come on in! Come on in! Miss Brooks, why the blankety-blank didn't you tell me it was Slade?"

"He didn't tell *me,"* the receptionist replied demurely, a dimple peeping at the corner of her red mouth.

"You were supposed to know anyway," boomed the sea lion. "Get my private bottle, and glasses — and pour one for yourself."

He turned and lumbered into his office. Slade glanced at the receptionist and saw that her beautiful brown eyes were following the broad back with real affection. Which was not strange, for it was said of Airley Gibbs by those who really knew him that if you pricked him with a pin you'd stab him to the heart. Slade knew it to be true; Airley Gibbs was a man who went about doing good.

The bottle and glasses were brought. After which, the receptionist softly closed the door. Gibbs proceeded to fill the glasses to the brim.

Slade often wondered where Airley Gibbs got his whiskey. The bottle bore no label but its content was distilled nectar.

"And what the devil brings you here?" Gibbs asked over the rim of his glass, his sea lion voice subdued to a thunder-gobbling out-of-a-cave rumble.

Slade told him, in detail. Gibbs listened attentively, his huge head cocked to one side.

"And so," the ranger concluded, "I was wondering if possibly some of the hired hands in this ruckus might have gotten out of control and are riding a side trail."

Gibbs pursed his cupid-bow mouth, put the tips of his plump fingers together.

"Walt, I don't think so, but it is not beyond the realm of possibility," he replied. "You know with the big fellows this sort of a row is strictly impersonal, the matter divorced from the individual. If Gates and the head of our outfit met on the street, they'd shake hands, have a drink together and talk over experiences and old times, and never mention business. Then next day they'd be fighting each other tooth and nail on the floor of the stock exchange. But that attitude doesn't always obtain where the hired hands, as you call them, are concerned. Sometimes they do get out of control and branch out on their own. It has happened before in such enterprises and will again. We have to work with such tools as we can get, and sometimes the tools prove faulty. To the best of my knowledge and belief, nothing like that is happening here at the present, but I am not infallible and I could be wrong."

"I see," Slade said thoughtfully. Abruptly he asked a question. "Do you know Berne Rader?" Gibbs nodded.

"Is he aligned with the Kountz interests?"

"He'd like to be," Gibbs replied. "He wants them to go ahead with plans to make Beaumont a deep-water port with a thirty-two foot channel and a turning basin fifteen hundred feet long and five hundred feet wide. And he wants to have a part in the project. He's shrewd and far-seeing, all right, but at present the interests are a bit cautious, what with railroad and pipeline competition, and are not at all sure that the project would pay off. So they turned down Rader's bid, for the moment, at least."

"How'd he take it, do you know?" Slade asked.

"He just smiled, and said that after all the whole business was rather petty, from his viewpoint. What the devil he meant by that, I don't know."

"I think I may," Slade replied slowly, "and if my hunch is a straight one, it *would* be petty business compared to what he has in mind, if he can put it across."

"Now what the devil do you mean by *that?*" Gibbs demanded.

"I'd rather not discuss it for the time being," Slade answered. "For, as I said, it's largely in the nature of a hunch. Later, perhaps. But I'll say this for Rader: In my opinion, the project he's urging on the interests is a sound one. Beaumont will eventually be a deep-water port, and a port of entry. It will be impossible for the railroad and the pipelines to handle all the business coming out of Beaumont and its environs and there will be plenty for water transportation. Keep that in mind for future reference, Airley; you might profit thereby."

"I will," the lawyer promised. "I have great faith in your judgment. Incidentally, Rader has gotten quite chummy with the bank officials here; they would stand to profit if the Kountz people go through with the project. I gather Rader has suggested that if our interests decline to further the project, that the banking interests here do so on their own hook. I've a notion they are flattered by the suggestion, but they know darn well they could never finance such an undertaking."

"Hardly," Slade agreed, "but it makes a good talking point for Rader."

"That's right," nodded Gibbs. "Well, let's go eat. Going to spend the night here?"

Slade shook his head. "I think I'll be ambling back to Beaumont," he replied. "Things have a habit of happening fast there of late."

"Forty miles of riding in one day is a considerable chore," grumbled Gibbs.

"Oh, I can take it, and so can Shadow," Slade answered lightly. "We'll jog along at an easy pace. Still lots of daylight, and there's a moon tonight."

Riding north, Slade felt that his trip to Port Arthur had not been altogether barren of results. He had confidence in Airley Gibbs' judgment and after what the lawyer told him he was inclined, to an extent, at least, to dismiss the idea that the wave of lawlessness plaguing the section might have birthed, in an incidental manner, from the row between the two big syndicates. Which would leave him free to devote his attention to other angles.

Also, what he had learned relative to that individual's activities had increased his interests in Berne Rader. It appeared Rader was gambling for big stakes, all right. And he felt that the manner in which he had accepted the refusal of the Kountz people to go along with his ideas was of interest. He rode on, planning future moves.

His next trip, he determined, would be his belated visit to Dunlap Jefferson's ranchhouse. His judgment of Jefferson must still be held in abeyance. Jefferson's fanatical hatred of the oil field and all it represented could not be lightly dismissed. And still to be explained, were the prints of riding boots in the neighborhood of the dynamited oil derrick. Perhaps on Jefferson's stamping grounds he might learn something that would tend to crystallize his opinion of the rancher.

Up to the present, Jefferson was his only logical suspect. In the back of his mind a nebulous theory was endeavoring to acquire form and substance; but until Jefferson was either focused on or eliminated, that theory must remain in a secondary position. For Jefferson was still the loose thread which refused to be woven into the pattern.

With a shrug of his broad shoulders he dismissed the whole aggravating affair and concentrated on enjoying the leisurely ride. The rangeland was drenched in golden sunshine and there was just a tang of Autumn in the air. The grass heads were assuming tips of amethyst and the deeper hollows were bronzed with the fading ferns. A fair land, Slade thought, with enough and more for all. If men would just cease striving for more than their allotted share and be content with the good that was already theirs!

Oh, well, perhaps that would come some day, and again the lion and the lamb lie down in peace together. But what about the sidewinders and other varmints? They and their human prototypes would very likely continue to thrive and make trouble for the other creatures that endeavored to live as they should. Slade chuckled and tweaked Shadow's ear. Shadow bared milk-white teeth and rolled an eye that promised retribution if the indignity was repeated. Slade chuckled again and they ambled on with perfect understanding.

He had covered something more than half the distance to Beaumont and the sun was low in the west when he paused on the crest of a rise to give Shadow a breather. From where he sat he could see the twin steel ribbons of the railroad a mile and better to the east, the right-of-way flanked by stands of tall and thick chaparral. Rolling a cigarette, he hooked one long leg over the saddle horn and sat gazing toward the shimmer of the rails. The smoke nearly finished, he was about ready to continue on his way when from the chaparral belt to the west of the rails appeared seven mounted men, pygmy men on pygmy horses at that distance. He idly watched them ride toward the railroad. When they reached the right-of-way, some forty or fifty yards from the growth, they pulled to a halt and dismounted. For a moment they clumped together then, climbing the slight embankment to the rails. Then they got very busy at something, just what Slade could not ascertain, the distance being too great.

"Now what are those jiggers up to?" he wondered aloud. He was pretty sure the men were not section hands; even at that distance they appeared to be wearing rangeland garb. And section hands or other maintenance workers would hardly be riding; they would use handcars as a means of transportation.

Soon the group ceased their activities, having apparently completed the chore, whatever that was. Six mounted and turned their horses' heads toward the chaparral. The seventh man followed on foot at the heels of his led horse; he appeared to be dragging something.

Now Slade's curiosity was fully aroused. He watched the chaparral swallow up the group, and although he sat for some minutes with his gaze fixed on the belt of growth, they did not reappear.

"Holed up in there, sure as blazes," he told Shadow. "Feller, I don't know what it's all about, but I've a hunch a little investigating might be in order. Let's go!"

Negotiating the far slope of the sag, Slade continued north for nearly a mile before turning east. When he reached the bristle of growth, he rode south in its shadow, every sense at hairtrigger alertness, for he had an uneasy premonition that everything was not as it should be; the activities of the mysterious group needed a little explaining. With what had they busied themselves on the railroad? He didn't know but intended to try and find out.

From the south, thin with distance, came the lonely wail of a locomotive whistle. Slade quickened Shadow's pace a little.

TWELVE

Bouncing about on the seatbox, fat old Tim Louden tooled his big locomotive along at a steady pace that ate up the miles. He was pulling a light train — two passenger coaches, a combination baggage-and-express car and twenty empty gondolas that would be loaded with scrap at Beaumont. The express car was next to the engine. He directed sarcastic remarks at the sweating fireman, who replied in kind. The head brakeman on his little perch in front of the fireman's seatbox expressed his opinion of both of them in terms that were far from flattering. It was all in good fun, however, and helped while away the time.

The brakeman peered through the left front window of the engine cab, narrowing his eyes.

"Say!" he exclaimed. "Looks like something burning there ahead, I see a wisp of smoke. Might be the end of a tie, smoldering."

Louden peered in turn. "Track's okay," he said. "Maybe the southbound dropped a spark. We'll report it when we get in. It —"

Without warning, the trickle of bluish smoke billowed to a yellowish cloud, shot through with spears of orange flame. The thunderous roar of the explosion rocked the cab and hurled Louden to the deck, even as he jammed the throttle shut and slammed on his emergency brake. The brakeman let out a terrified yell, which was his last. Into the tangle of twisted rails, splintered ties and the yawning crater torn in the right-of-way by the dynamite, plunged the locomotive. Over onto its side it crashed and rolled down the low embankment, steam bellowing from broken pipes, snapping loose from the express car which slanted half into the smoky hole but remained upright. Two of the gondolas were derailed. The passenger coaches in the rear, next to the caboose, stayed on the iron.

From the bristle of growth flanking the right-of-way leaped seven men who raced toward the wreck. A volley of shots directed at the passenger coaches in the rear sent heads popping back in windows.

Something hurtled through the air, trailing a spurtle of sparks. A second booming explosion quivered the air as the stick of dynamite struck the express car door, blowing it to fragments.

Into the express car swarmed three of the outlaws. The other four continued to throw lead toward the passenger cars to guarantee no interference from that source. One callously took a shot at the fireman, who was crawling away from the overturned locomotive, trailing a broken leg. He collapsed in a moaning heap.

Wisps of smoke were spiraling up from the wooden cab of the engine, where old Tim Louden lay helpless.

From inside the express car sounded a single shot, then a clang of metal on metal. The raid was proceeding with the precision of a smoothly oiled machine.

Not quite! There was a crashing in the brush, and from the chaparral belt stormed a great black horse, nostrils flaring, eyes rolling, his glossy mane tossing in the wind of his passing. The knotted reins lay on his arching neck and his tall rider had an unleathered Colt in each hand.

With a rattling crash, both of Walt Slade's guns let go. Two of the robbers, who had whirled to face him, went down before that thundering volley. The other two, ducking, weaving, answered the ranger shot for shot. But Shadow was also swerving and weaving, his rider an elusive and ever-shifting target, and none of the bullets found a mark.

The three robbers in the express car came leaping to the ground, their guns blazing. Slugs buzzed about the embattled ranger like disturbed bees.

Slade knew it was but a matter of seconds till one drilled home; the odds were too great. He snapped a shot under Shadow's neck and another of the outlaws went whirling around and around with a bullet through his shoulder. The hammer of one gun clicked on an empty shell; there was but a single unexploded cartridge in the other.

But now men, pistols in their hands, were racing from the passenger coaches toward the pandemonium of bellowing steam, crackling flames and blazing guns. With whoops and yells they opened fire.

A voice bawled a command. The outlaws fled madly for the brush. The passengers, with plenty of enthusiasm but little aim, banged away at them. Slade, frantically stuffing cartridges into his empty Colts, started to race in pursuit. But as he passed the overturned engine he saw the bulky form of old Tim Louden lying on the sloping deck of the cab, which was now burning fiercely, flames playing around him.

Jerking Shadow to a slithering halt, Slade swung from the saddle and sped to the steam-spouting locomotive. Shielding his face from the flames with one arm, he plunged into the withering heat and choking smoke, managed to get a hold on the old engineer's collar and, after a terrific struggle, dragged him to safety. Cradling the heavy form in his arms, he staggered away from the crackling cab.

And then to make matters complete, the locomotive boiler exploded with a sodden boom. Slade was hurled to the ground, still clinging to Louden. Several of the approaching passengers were knocked off their feet. Nobody was seriously hurt, but the air was blue with cursing. And through the diminishing uproar, Slade heard a distant crashing in the brush where the thwarted outlaws were hightailing it away from there.

Rather shakily, Slade struggled to his knees and strove to ascertain the extent of the engineer's injuries. Louden had a swelling lump on the side of his head, but Slade's sensitive fingers could discover no indications of fracture.

"Not hurt much, should be coming out of it soon," he told the passengers who were crowding around, volleying questions. "But you gentlemen got into action at just the right time. Did they kill the fireman?"

"He's settin' up, cussin'," somebody replied.

Slade got to his feet and walked to where the fireman was cherishing his injured leg and indulging in vivid profanity.

"Just the little bone busted, I think," he panted. "Nope, the slug didn't get me; I flopped down and played 'possum. Poor Phillips, the shack, got it, though; crushed between the cab and the boilerhead. He never had a chance. I was pitched out the window. Feller, you're a wonder! You got two of the skunks. How's Tim, the hogger?"

"He'll be okay," Slade replied. "I'll see what I can do for you in a minute. Where's the conductor?"

"Here he comes!" somebody shouted.

The conductor hurried forward. With him came the express messenger, swabbing at his bloody head with a handkerchief.

"Creased me," he answered Slade's question. "Knocked me out for a few minutes. Reckon they figured I was dead. Lucky for me they did, I reckon, the snake-blooded wind spiders!"

"I'll look at that cut shortly," Slade said. He turned to the conductor.

"Got a portable telegraph instrument with

you?" he asked.

"Yes, one in the caboose," the conductor replied.

"Get it and we'll hook it up and get through to Port Arthur. You can send enough to tell them to dispatch the wreck train and a doctor? If you can't, I think I can."

"I can manage, if we can get up a pole and hook her," the conductor answered.

"I'll make it up the pole," Slade said. "I wonder whose bright notion it was to place that express car between the engine and a score of steel gondolas, and why? It's a wonder it wasn't smashed to splinters."

"I dunno," said the conductor. "We were pulling out of the yards when they stopped us and told us to couple it on that way. It was standing on a spur and all we had to do was cut the engine loose, grab it and tie it on. Didn't take us three minutes. I dunno why they did it, but that was orders."

"I see," Slade said thoughtfully. "Go get that instrument."

He turned to the express messenger. "Well?" he asked.

The messenger evidently understood. He shot Slade a keen glance and nodded.

"Combination knob knocked off the safe but that was as far as they got before you landed on 'em," he said in low tones as the conductor hurried away. "Nigh onto a hundred thousand dollars in oil field payroll money in that safe. Supposed to be a dead secret; not even the train crew knew about it. Had the car picked up the last minute. Precaution against a leak. Looks like there was a leak, though, or those hellions were just guessing."

"I don't think they were guessing," Slade said. "Somebody knew how to handle dynamite, too; the timing was perfect. I'll tie up your head — bandages and salve in my saddle pouches. Then I'll have a look at the fireman. Perhaps I can set the bone and splint the leg; that is, if there are no indications of a compound fracture. In which case he'll have to wait for the doctor; I prefer not to tackle that."

"I've a notion you'd handle that, too, just as well as the doctor could," replied the messenger. "Look after that tallowpot first. My head's just scratched."

The chore of caring for the injured fireman proved simpler than Slade anticipated.

"I think the bone is only cracked, not really fractured," he told the tallowpot after a brief examination. He quickly manufactured a couple of splints out of shoots cut from the chaparral and bound them into place.

"That's a devil of a sight better," said the fireman, with a sigh of relief as he gratefully accepted the cigarette Slade rolled for him. "You sure you ain't a doctor?"

Some salve, a pad and a bandage took care of the express messenger, by which time old Tim Louden, the engineer, was sitting up, rather groggy but able to vividly express his opinion of the whole situation.

Before Slade finished with his patients, the conductor arrived with the telegraph instrument. Slade hooked the wires to his belt and went up a nearby pole hand over hand.

"Will you look at that!" marveled the conductor. "That big jigger don't know his own strength. He's goin' up that pole with his hands, like an average climber would go up a rope. Who in blazes is he?"

"Don't you know?" replied a passenger. "That's *El Halcon,* the owlhoot."

"Owlhoot, my — ankle!" snorted the conductor. "He saved Tim from getting burned up and saved whatever the devil's in the express car safe. And look at those two skunks laying over there on the ground. *Them's* owlhoots! He's a bully boy with a glass eye, for me."

"Me, too," said somebody else. The passenger who made the remark suddenly found himself the recipient of indignant glares from every direction.

"I didn't mean nothing," he mumbled. "I was just saying what people say."

"Blankety-blank terrapin-brained horned toads who don't know what the halifax they're talking about say too blasted much!" bawled old Tim Louden, hobbling forward rubbing his bruised knob. "I'm in the notion of punchin' somebody in the nose!"

The informative passenger made himself scarce.

Slade quickly hooked up the instrument and the conductor fumbled a message over the wires.

"They'll be on their way pronto," he announced as he closed the key. "They're wiring Sheriff Colton — we're in Jefferson County now, you know — telling him to head down here. Guess that takes care of everything we can do. Come on back to the crummy, feller, and we'll have coffee and a snack. My name's Arbaugh, Gordon Arbaugh. I didn't catch your handle."

Slade supplied it and they shook hands.

Before repairing to the caboose with the hospitable conductor, Slade gave the bodies of the slain outlaws a careful once-over, with the conductor present. They were ornery looking specimens with nothing outstanding about them.

"Border gun-for-hire sidewinders," he commented. "Let's see what they've got on them."

The pockets turned out nothing of significance other than a rather large sum of money, nearly packeted.

"Looks like they might have gotten their pay in advance," he remarked, tossing the packets aside.

"If the train crew should happen to pick it up to sort of even out for what they went through, I reckon it would be in the nature of retributive justice, and anyhow the county treasury isn't particularly in need of it," he added, turning his back and sauntering toward the chaparral thickets, where he hoped to locate the horses the pair rode. He heard the conductor chuckle and when he glanced around, the money had disappeared.

However, a search of the growth revealed no trace of the horses. Evidently they had galloped after the others when the surviving outlaws fled.

"Brands might have told us something," he remarked to the conductor. "Let's go get that coffee."

An hour later the wreck train arrived and began cleaning up the mess. Another hour and a half elapsed before the sheriff and his posse put in an appearance. With him were ex-governor Hogg and Jim Roche. Slade drew Hogg aside.

"There was a bad leak somewhere," he said. "The hellions knew the money was in that safe. Even the expedient of coupling the express car on at the last moment ahead of those gondolas, where it had no business to be, did not fool them. They knew right where to look."

"Would appear you are right," replied Hogg. "The boys felt that it was the safest way to send the money, considering the things that have been happening of late, and the bank people went along with the idea. Somebody talked out of turn, all right, with the wrong pair of ears listening; maybe we can learn who."

"Maybe," Slade agreed, but without conviction.

"Well, you saved the money, all right, but how in blazes did you happen to be on the spot at just the right time?"

"Very largely a lucky break," Slade explained, with a brief account of what happened.

"When I saw those devils working over something on the right-of-way I got curious, and ambled over this way," he concluded. "I was pretty close when the dynamite cut loose and figured a mite of investigation was in order."

"Quite an investigation," Hogg remarked dryly. "And you tackled the whole bunch of them! By all odds you should have been killed."

"I very likely would have been if it weren't for the passengers lending a hand," Slade said. "They're not much as marksmen but they sure kicked up one heck of a racket and scared the hellions off. I'm thankful that most everybody in this section packs a gun, even if he doesn't know how to use it."

Hogg shook his head in wordless admiration. "You're the limit!" he declared. "Looks like you have some particular devil who looks after his own. Here comes the sheriff."

"Don't reckon there's any sense in trying to trail those sidewinders in the dark," Colton said as he joined them.

"None at all," Slade agreed. "They could be darn near to Mexico by now, if they kept going at the speed they left here. Well, everything appears to be under control and we might as well head for Beaumont."

"Guess so," nodded Colton. "Plenty of folks to take care of any more trouble."

"There won't be, not tonight," Slade said. The sheriff nodded again. "I'll arrange to have those two carcasses sent to Beaumont on the train, along with what's left of that poor brakeman; every bone in his body was busted. Plain snake-blooded murder."

Slade did not comment, but his eyes were even colder than usual as he glanced at where the brakeman's broken body lay covered with a blanket.

The quiet Roche spoke for the first time. "I repeat," he said, "Mr. Slade is certainly full of surprises. I wonder what next?"

"He'll pull a real one on you sooner or later, I've a notion," Hogg said, with a chuckle.

"Nothing will surprise me any more," Roche declared emphatically.

It was late when they arrived at Beaumont, and Slade found himself quite weary; it had been a hectic day.

"And now what?" asked the sheriff.

"Now I'm going to bed," the ranger replied. "Tomorrow I figure to ride to the Diamond ranchhouse and have a little gab with *Senor* Jefferson."

Sheriff Colton shot him a quick glance, but did not comment; nor did he ask any questions.

"Don't forget the handcuffs," Hogg said, sotto voce, as the sheriff turned away.

Slade grinned, and did not reply.

THIRTEEN

The following morning, Slade rode west by slightly north through the golden sunshine, following a well-defined track that he knew would lead him to the Dunlap Jefferson ranchhouse. The Diamond-brand horse trotted complacently beside Shadow.

Slade rode warily, although with his Winchester ready to hand and Shadow between his thighs, he didn't anticipate any trouble he couldn't take care of. Just the same, he was taking no chances.

The first person Slade met when he arrived at the Diamond ranchhouse, a fine old casa set in a grove of wide-spread oaks, was Steve Rafferty, the old puncher with whom he talked in Beaumont the day Cliff Tevis' body was returned to the ranchhouse for burial. Rafferty's greeting was warm.

"Hoped you'd make it," said Rafferty. "Light off and cool your saddle. Where'd you get the critter?" He gestured to the led horse.

"Picked him up at the Big Thicket the other day," Slade said, as he dismounted. "Figured he belonged to your outfit, so I brought him along."

Rafferty scrutinized the horse, and shook his head. "Not one of ours," he disclaimed. "We haven't got a skewbald in our remuda. Haven't had one for a long time."

"Wearing your brand," Slade pointed out.

Rafferty walked closer, and stared. "Darned if it ain't!" he exclaimed. "Now what in blazes!" He peered at the brand mark, traced it with his forefinger.

"Say!" he exclaimed. "This burn was done with a slick-iron!"

Slade nodded. "Do you use a running iron here?" he asked casually.

Rafferty shook his head definitely. "Not one on the place," he declared. "The boss won't stand for 'em." He studied the brand some more.

"Not a very old burn," he decided. "Not old at all. Now who in blazes would do such a thing, and why?"

There was no doubt in Slade's mind but that Rafferty's bewilderment was genuine, which was what he had anticipated. He shrugged his broad shoulders.

"Your guess is as good as mine," he said. "Should be better, seeing as you are acquainted with the section while I am not."

"Doesn't seem to help me any," grumbled Rafferty. "It's got me plumb flabbergasted. The Irish are supposed to have the 'second sight,' but it sure ain't working this time. Well, let's go up to the house, I'll call somebody to take care of your critter, and that misfit, if you don't want him. You found him, and finders are keepers."

He let out a bellow and a wrangler appeared. "Put 'em both up," ordered Rafferty, who, Slade gathered, had taken over the chore of range boss since the death of Cliff Tevis. The wrangler nodded and approached Shadow, who laid back his ears.

"It's okay, Shadow, go along with him," Slade said.

Rafferty gazed admiringly at the great black horse. "Never saw a finer cayuse," he said, "and I'm darned if I don't believe he understood what you said."

"He did," Slade replied briefly, as Shadow allowed the wrangler to take his bridle and ambled along docilely.

Slade expected to find Dunlap Jefferson in the ranchhouse. Instead, a girl was standing by the window when they entered the big, tastefully furnished living room. She was a rather tall girl with auburn hair and very large dark eyes. Her red lips smiled pleasantly as she turned to greet them.

"Pat," said Rafferty, "this is Slade, the feller I was telling you about. Slade, I want you to know Miss Pat, the boss' daughter."

"How are you, Mr. Slade?" the girl said, extending a slender sun-golden hand. "Steve has been singing your praises ever since he met you."

"Ebullience and flowery descriptions are to be expected from anybody by the name of Rafferty," Slade smiled, bowing over her hand with courtly grace.

"The Irish judge with the heart, not the head, that's why they're never wrong," said Rafferty.

"I've usually found Steve's judgment sound," the girl remarked. "He never disappoints me."

"Didn't this time, did I?" asked Rafferty. "Old Steve knows how to pick 'em."

The girl laughed merrily, her even teeth flashing white against the red of her lips. Slade decided that Miss Patricia Jefferson was not at all hard to look at; she had inherited her father's good looks, all right. And he suspected there was more than average intelligence under the curly reddish hair.

Rafferty headed for the kitchen. "Going

to tell the cook to rattle his hocks," he said over his shoulder. "Having company always makes me hungry." With a chuckle, he ducked through the door and out of sight.

"Have a chair, Mr. Slade," the girl invited. She sat down opposite him, crossed a very shapely pair of legs, cupped her little round white chin in a pink palm and regarded him fixedly in silence for a moment.

"Really you don't seem to be the terrible person my father says you are," she said at length. "I'm inclined to believe Steve has nearer the right of it."

"Perhaps Steve is prejudiced," Slade smiled.

"And I fear my father is also prejudiced," she replied quietly. "Your being a friend of Mr. Hogg and Mr. Gates inclines him to be suspicious of you. He is not particularly fond of the oil people."

"So I gathered," Slade agreed dryly.

"I think his attitude is foolish," she said. "But old people are set in their ways and all too often live in the past, and it is hard to change them."

"Yes," Slade again agreed, guardedly. He wished to learn just what Miss Patricia's attitude toward the controversy really was before committing himself in any way. She seemed to read his thought, for she smiled and shook her head.

"I do not uphold him in his attitude," she said. "I don't agree that the oil strike is harmful to the rangeland, but I can appreciate his feeling in the matter. He truly believes it himself, of that you can be assured; a more honest man never lived. He is stubborn and, as I said, set in his ways, but show him he is wrong and he is quick to change. I've seen him reverse himself very quickly when shown he was in error. Also, I wish to assure you that *he* is not the terrible person the oil people say he is. He is not responsible for the things that have happened at the field. His methods are direct, never underhanded."

Slade thought that Dunlap Jefferson was fortunate in having so charming and able an advocate as this young daughter of his, but he held his peace.

In fact, although she didn't know it, Miss Patricia was getting a taste of Walt Slade's amazing ability to say nothing and let the other person do all the talking.

Perhaps she did sense it, in a way, for she abruptly looked baffled and relapsed into silence. A ghost of a smile touching his lips, Slade waited, also silent.

Finally, being impulsive by nature, she

could stand it no longer.

"I wish I knew what you really believe," she said.

"Even though it might perturb you?"

"Yes. Because I'd know it was the truth."

"Thank you," Slade said. "But remember, a hair perhaps divides the false and true."

"What do you mean by that?" she asked.

"I mean," he replied, "that while truth is static and cannot be affected by argument, the individual's interpretation of the truth may be fallacious. The human brain is prone to error."

A little pucker appeared between her delicate black brows. "I think I understand," she said. "One may be sincere in one's belief and still be wrong."

"Exactly."

"Then you won't tell me what you believe?"

"You haven't asked me," Slade smiled.

"Well, I will ask you," she retorted. "Do you believe my father is responsible for what happened at the field?"

"Not directly."

"Indirectly?"

"I don't know, yet," Slade answered. "A child playing with matches does not intend to loose a destructive force, but it may do just that."

"I see," she said thoughtfully. "You mean that my father's attitude may have influenced others and caused them to go to undue lengths?"

Slade didn't mean exactly that, but decided it was close enough to pass. He nodded.

"I'm glad you told me," she said, adding contritely, "I've put you through a regular cross-examination. I'm sorry, but I really did wish to know what you thought. No more questions, I promise. I'll play for you; that will keep my mouth shut — for a while, anyhow." She crossed to a magnificent grand piano that stood near one wall, and sat down on the stool.

She played quite well. Slade smoked and listened till Steve Rafferty stuck his head in the door and bellowed, "Come and get it!" Together they trooped into the dining room to a really excellent meal.

While they were eating, the beat of a horse's hoofs sounded outside. A moment later, Dunlap Jefferson entered the room. He stared at Slade in surprise, but quickly recovered his aplomb.

"So!" he said. "Decided to come and sing for me, and sign up?"

"I'll sing for you, if you really wish me to," Slade said, with a smile.

Miss Pat glanced at Slade, then at her father. "You didn't tell me he could sing," she said reproachfully.

"Guess I didn't," Jefferson replied cheerfully as he sat down. "I'll let you judge for yourself."

"Dad sings quite well himself," Patricia said. "I play his accompaniments. That's why he bought me this wonderful piano."

Jefferson grinned, and winked at Slade.

Fourteen

In the living room, after Slade had smoked a couple of cigarettes and Jefferson had knocked out his pipe, Patricia glanced expectantly at the ranger.

"Please," she said, gesturing to the piano.

Slade sat down at the instrument and ran his fingers over the keys. With the touch of a master he played a soft prelude, then sang.

Follow the trail of the thundering herd
With the Texas stars above,
Through the rising mist
From the brown earth kissed
By the frost in its Autumn love!
Follow the trail of dust and dreams
Where the prairie roses bloom,
Where the coyote prowls
And the lone wolf howls
To his mate in the star-burned gloom!
Follow the gray of the Pecos Trail,
On to the rising sun,

Till the Sabine gleams
In the first red beams,
And the West and the East are one!

The music ended with a crash of booming chords, and Slade sat smiling at his entranced audience.

"And you let me annoy you with my tinkling!" Patricia said accusingly. "I'll never again touch a piano in your presence."

"I knew enough not to do any bellerin' with him around," chuckled her father. "The singingest man in the whole Southwest, they call him," he said to his daughter. "Guess that's about the right of it."

"Do you know who wrote the song?" Pat asked. "It's beautiful."

"A cowhand threw it together, to sing the cows to sleep," Slade replied carelessly, not mentioning the fact that he was the cowboy composer in question.

"I guess he never had it published," said Pat. "Otherwise I'd have recognized it, for it would have taken the country by storm."

"Give us another, son," said Jefferson.

Slade sang several more for them, and played a couple of selections. Then the hands trooped in for dinner and the house became a bedlam. Pat went to the kitchen to give the cook a hand, leaving Slade and her father in the living room. Slade turned to his host.

"Mind walking over to the stable with me, sir?" he asked. "Something there I wish to show you."

"Not in the least," replied Jefferson, rising to his feet. "What is it, that horse of yours? I've seen him. He's a beauty."

"No, not my horse," Slade replied. "One the ownership of which I'm anxious to establish."

Jefferson looked puzzled, but did not ask more questions as they walked to the stable. There, Slade pointed to the stalled horse. Jefferson gazed at it for a moment. Slade gazed at Jefferson.

"Don't recall ever seeing the critter before," the ranchowner replied.

"Take a look at the brand," Slade suggested, his eyes still hard on the other's face, noting every change of expression.

Jefferson did as requested. "What the devil!" he sputtered. "A Diamond, my brand." He peered closer. "Say, this burn was run with a slick-iron!" he exclaimed.

"You don't use a running iron?" Slade asked, intently watching the ranchowner's reactions.

"Haven't had one on the place for years," Jefferson replied. "I don't approve of them.

Where did you get this animal?"

"Up at the Big Thicket," Slade replied.

"Who was riding it?"

"To the best of my belief, a member of the Twilight Riders," Slade answered.

Jefferson's eyes widened. His jaw sagged a little. Slade concluded that if his bewilderment was not genuine, he was one darn good actor.

"The Twilight Riders!" Jefferson repeated.

"Yes," Slade said. "This makes three altogether. Two more were mavericking around up there on the prairie. Incidentally, Sheriff Colton saw the first one, which was ridden by the drygulcher who very nearly did for both of us."

"The devil he did!" exclaimed Jefferson. "Why didn't he mention it to me?"

"Because I asked him to mention it to nobody, and persuaded him not to take the horse to town and show it around," Slade answered.

Jefferson seemed to understand what was implied. "That was thoughtful, and considerate," he said. "Why did you do it?" he suddenly asked.

Having carefully studied Jefferson's reactions, Slade arrived at a decision.

"Because I didn't see any sense in creating unnecessary comment and causing people to jump to perhaps a wrong conclusion," he said. "You've made enough enemies with your arrogance, bullheaded contrariness and utter disregard for the rights and good of others."

Dunlap Jefferson was little used to being spoken to in such a tone of voice, but something in the cold, steady eyes to which he had to raise his own to meet, gave him pause.

"I can't see as you have any right to talk to me in this fashion," he mumbled.

"Apparently there are a number of things you can't see," Slade retorted. "A long period of authority and immunity to restrictions in this section appears to have imbued you with the fallacious belief that you are above and beyond the rules of decency and live-and-let-live. I assure you it is not so. Keep on the way you are going and you may have to be enlightened as Pharaoh was enlightened."

This castigation left the Diamond owner's eyes a bit glassy, and he appeared for the moment bereft of speech.

"By your loco talk and actions," Slade continued, "you have played into the hands of a smart, dangerous and ruthless man who is out to feather his own nest regardless of who gets hurt in the process. And you may well end up as one of the victims. You are pretty well hated down at the oil field, and to an extent in Beaumont, and in some quarters patience is wearing mighty thin. Let one of those slick-ironed horses fall into the wrong hands or the brands be noted when the Twilight Riders are pulling one of their depredations with murder as a side line, and conceivably a necktie party of a few hundred might ride over this way. Such things have happened."

Jefferson winced a little at this ominous prediction. He found his tongue.

"Slade, I can't make you out," he complained. "Everybody says you're an owlhoot —"

Slade smiled for the first time since entering the stable. "Not everybody," he corrected.

"Well, a lot have said it," Jefferson insisted defensively. "But you don't act like one and you don't talk like one. I'll admit you've given me something of a jolt. What do you figure I should do?"

"First off, pull in your horns and stop making big medicine," Slade replied. "You can't talk the oil field away, but you can needlessly rile a lot of people. Don't interfere with anybody who wants to drill on state land over to the west, even though you consider it open range that should be reserved for the cattlemen. Let them waste their time and money on it if they are of a mind to. And," he added as an afterthought, "don't sell an inch of your own land to anybody, no matter what you're offered. And if somebody should happen to make you an attractive offer for some of your holding, you would be doing me a big favor by letting me know at once who makes the offer."

Jefferson again looked bewildered; but he evidently concluded that if he asked a question he wouldn't get an answer. Which was so.

"Okay," he said, "I'll take your advice, in everything. Let's go back to the house and get some coffee; I feel the need of some."

Walking back to the house, Slade felt that his visit to the Diamond ranch had not been altogether barren of results. A peace officer's first duty is to prevent trouble if possible, and he believed that by cooling down Dunlap Jefferson a mite, he had taken a stride in that direction.

Halfway up the slight rise that led to the great ranchhouse, Jefferson paused to gaze across the wide rangeland, gold and green in the yellow sunlight.

"A fine holding, don't you think?" he observed.

Slade turned to face the ranchowner. "Yes, very fine," he said softly, his deep voice all music. "Very fine. The kind of a holding that makes a man thankful for the good that has come to him. That makes him ready to extend a helping hand to others, to help others also gain some of the good this great land of ours has to offer. That makes him want to share. That makes him want to see others attain happiness, and peace, and freedom from care. That causes him to bow his head humbly and say with the Psalmist of old, 'Thou preparest a table before me in the presence of mine enemies . . . my cup runneth over.' "

Dunlap Jefferson's face flushed darkly red as the words struck home. His glance wavered, and once again he seemed bereft of speech. Then abruptly his eyes met *El Halcon's* squarely.

"Slade," he said, "Tom Colton says you're the hardest man to talk to he ever met. I've got something to add to that: You're the hardest man to be talked to *by, I* ever met. You can scare the devil out of a man by just talking to him, and you can make him feel lower than a snake's belly, by just talking to him. How do you do it?"

The little devils of laughter suddenly danced in the depths of Slade's eyes.

"Perhaps I just call to mind what that man has been thinking all along but wouldn't admit it to himself," he replied.

"Yes, that could be it," Jefferson said slowly. "Oh, heck! Let's go get that coffee."

When they entered the living room, Pat was there. But instead of a very pretty dress, she now wore Levis, a soft woolen shirt, open at the throat, trim little spurred riding boots, and a "J.B." set jauntily on her red curls.

"Mr. Slade," she said, "I'm going to take a mean advantage of you; I'm going to ask you to take me riding. I want to show you over our spread."

"I'll be delighted to," Slade replied. "I'll get my horse."

"I anticipated the favor and ordered my own sent over," said Pat. "I felt you'd prefer to get the rig on yours yourself."

"That's right," Slade agreed, and headed for the door.

"Coffee'll be ready when you get back," Jefferson called after him.

Pat turned to her father. "What's the matter, Dad?" she asked. "You look — subdued."

"I am," growled Jefferson. "I've just listened to two of the stiffest talkings to I ever got in my life, and I couldn't find a word to answer. He's the limit!"

"Outlaw, eh?" Pat said, with a little trill of laughter. "He's about as much an outlaw as Steve Rafferty."

"Then what the devil is he?" her father demanded in exasperated tones.

"I don't know," his daughter replied blithely, "except he's the handsomest man I ever met, and the most charming. And that voice!"

"He takes everybody in tow!" groaned Jefferson. "He's got Tom Colton hypnotized. Jim Hogg and Bet-a-Million Gates swear by him. Terry Sullivan swears he's the finest thing that ever wore shoe leather, and Rafferty hadn't talked with him for two minutes till he was following him around like a pet dog."

Pat was suddenly serious. "Dad," she said, "when he walked into the dining room, old Manuel, our cook, crossed himself and bowed his head as to a shrine. You didn't notice, but I did. I asked him why he did it, and he said, '*Senora,* when *El Halcon* enters, it is as if Our Lord sits to break bread with us. When *El Halcon* comes, the good rejoice, the evil tremble.'"

"I understand that," said Jefferson. "I sort of had the shakes myself a little while back, but I feel better now. Guess anybody does when those eyes laugh at him. When they don't laugh, they seem to be hunting out all the dark places inside you to show you how black those places really are. But when they laugh, they make you feel good all over. What else did Manuel have to say about him?"

"I asked him who he was and where did he come from?" Pat replied slowly. "You know, Manuel, like many Mexicans, talks in poetry or very near it when he is moved. He said, 'He is *El Halcon.* Whence comes the wind to bring the rain that makes the earth rejoice? Where trouble is, or sorrow, or evil, there is *El Halcon.* When he departs, like the kindly wind he leaves behind him peace, and happiness, and content.' That's all I could get out of him."

"Manuel may have something there," Jefferson said thoughtfully.

"I'm not so sure of it, in every case," Pat replied enigmatically, and was out the door before he could ask her what the devil she meant.

Slade was just halting the horses beside the veranda. Pat regarded him with laughing eyes. "Will you hold my stirrup for me?" she asked demurely.

"Nope, there's a better way," Slade replied. His hands encircled her trim waist and the next instant she was in the saddle.

"Good heavens!" she exclaimed breathlessly. "I don't believe you have any idea how strong you are! I am not a child in weight."

"Not far from it," was the cheerful reply as Slade mounted and they rode out of the yard.

"Oh! We forgot all about the coffee," she exclaimed.

"It'll keep till we get back," Slade answered. "Let's go! Which way?"

"If you don't mind," she said, "I'd like to ride up to the Big Thicket. I love the Thicket; it's beautiful in there, and so peaceful under the great trees."

Slade hesitated for a moment before replying. Oh, what the devil! The chances of meeting somebody he wouldn't wish to with her along was one in a thousand.

"Okay," he agreed, but felt constrained to add, "It's not always as safe in there as it appears to be."

"I know, there are lots of animals and things, but I don't mind them. I did have to shoot a big rattler's head off once, but that was all," she said, touching the gun swinging at her hip.

"Shot its head off?" Slade remarked, interested. "You must be a good shot. A rattler's head, which is vibrating when it's angry, is not easy to hit."

"I am," she said. "It sort of runs in the family. Dad is an extremely good shot. He's not fast on the draw, but he never misses what he aims at. He says his father was a quick-draw man and a dead shot."

"Guess he had to be in his day," Slade commented. "This section was sort of woolly back in those days. Not exactly tame now, but not what it was then. Okay, the Big Thicket it is, but here's hoping you don't have to shoot any snakes today."

"I hope not," she said, "but I will if necessary." A remark Slade would later remember.

FIFTEEN

They rode mostly in silence, reveling in the panorama of beauty spread before their eyes. Everywhere were clumps of sleek cows bearing the Diamond brand, conclusive evidence that Dunlap Jefferson was a man of substance and bountifully endowed in this world's goods. Slade, however, despite the loveliness spread about him and the charming companion by his side, kept a close watch on their immediate and distant surroundings; his vigilance never relaxed.

About midafternoon the Big Thicket loomed on the northeastern horizon, dark, sombre, mysterious, its tangled sprawl seeming to hide an ancient mystery and to hint of secret evil done amid its gloom. A last remnant of the days when this was a wild land, the domain of savage beasts and still more savage men. And, Slade reflected, the predatory still roamed in the still fastnesses over there where the great trees shouldered the sky and the bristling under-growth cloaked that which it is not good for man to look upon.

They reached the wall of growth and entered it. With the plainsman's uncanny sense of distance and direction, Slade had no difficulty locating the trail by which he had reached the prairie from Uncle Eben's cabin.

"Being as you must prowl the Thicket, I'm going to take you to visit a friend of mine," he told Pat. "He'll dish up a prime sur-rounding for us, which I figure we can use about now."

"I'm sure I can, I'm starved," she replied. "Mr. Slade, you seem to have friends every-where, in the most unusual places."

"Friends are where you find them," he returned, "and by the way, my friends call me Walt."

"My acquaintances call me Patricia or Miss Patricia, but my *friends* find Pat shorter and easier to pronounce — Walt," she replied, with a sideways glance of her big eyes.

"Okay, Pat," he chuckled. "That is, if I can presume to be more than an acquain-tance."

"What you presume to be is largely up to

you," she answered, with a significance that was not altogether lost on him.

"That, to a man who, for all you know, has a price on his head!" he teased.

Miss Patricia's reaction was an undignified sniff. "More likely a man who has an untold number of women's paws reaching for him," she retorted.

"That's flattering, in a way," he replied, with a laugh, "but hardly the case."

Pat did not look convinced.

"Oh, well," she said, "I suppose there's safety in numbers. But watch out, your fate may catch up with you sooner or later."

"I'm beginning to think it may be sooner," he chuckled. All the reply he got was another sideways glance.

They rode on, through the rustling red- and yellow-tinted forest, under amber or scarlet spreading arches. All about them was silence, the sweet, restful silence of nature.

And yet there was no lack of life — the whole wide wood was full of it. Now it was a lithe, furtive weasel which shot across the trail upon some errand of its own; then it was a wildcat that squatted upon the outlying branch of an oak and peered at the travelers with a yellow and dubious eye. Once it was a wild sow which scuttled out of the growth with two young piglets at her heels. Birds flitted back and forth in the thickets, with an occasional musical note. Here it was, Slade thought, as in the beginning, when He created from the sacred "dust." And the picture was complete — a man, a maid, and a Garden!

Finally they reached the edge of the cultivated clearing where Uncle Eben Prescott's cabin stood. Slade jerked Shadow to a standstill, halting his companion's mount with a quick hand on the bit iron. Near the cabin door, which stood ajar, were three horses with hanging reins. A glance told him that they bore the Diamond brand.

"Hold it!" he whispered to Pat. "Something wrong here, I'm afraid."

Even as he spoke, from the cabin came a rumble of voices and a cry of pain.

Slade slipped to the ground. "Stay here," he ordered, and crossed the clearing with quick, lithe steps, his eyes fixed on the windows. As he reached the door, there was another cry of pain and a brutal laugh. He flung the door open, his eyes narrowing to adjust to the comparative gloom of the cabin.

On one of the bunks, his wrists and his ankles bound, lay Uncle Eben. Over him bent three men, one holding a glowing branding iron. They whirled with startled exclamations as the door banged against the wall.

"Look out!" one yelled. "It's him!" The cabin exploded to the roar of guns.

Ducking, Slade shot with both hands, holding high against the danger of hitting the colored man on the bunk. Blood streamed down his face from where a slug ripped the skin of his cheek. His hat flew off as two bullets slammed through it. Spurts of flame lanced the gushing smoke clouds. The targets across the room were but shifting shadows.

Two men were down, sprawled on the puncheon floor. The third suddenly stood stock still and lined his barrel with Slade's breast. The ranger pulled both triggers, and the hammers clicked on empty shells!

A gun blazed over Slade's shoulder. The outlaw whirled about as if smashed by a mighty fist. He gave a choking cry and fell. His body twitched for a moment and lay still.

Slade peered through the drifting smoke, automatically reloading his Colts. Looked like everything was under control. He turned to face Pat, who stood with her smoking gun in her hand, her eyes wide with horror.

"Oh!" she gasped. "I killed him!"

"Yes, and thanks for a mighty good chore," Slade replied. "I thought for a moment my number was up. It would have been if it hadn't been for you."

She swayed toward him, as if about to fall. He slipped the guns in their sheaths, caught her in his arms and held her close. She clung to him, sobbing convulsively.

"I'm sorry," she whimpered, "but I never shot anybody before."

"You made a darn good beginning," Slade told her cheerfully as he patted her bright hair. "Take it easy, now, while I see what they did to Uncle Eben."

A couple of slashes with his knife freed the colored man, who sat up, flexing his fingers.

"Hurt much?" Slade asked anxiously.

"Nope, not much," said Uncle Eben. "They burned my wrists a couple of times, but not bad, not bad. A little grease will take care of 'em. They were tryin' to make me send for you to come up here; they'd have been layin' for you. I wouldn't do it."

"You're a real *amigo*," Slade said, patting his shoulder. "And a lot of man. Wonder how the devil they connected you with me?"

"That little one over there," said Uncle Eben, gesturing to the bodies, "is a full-blooded Kiowa Injun or I'm a heap mistook.

The Kiowas are just about the best trackers in Texas. Guess he tracked you here from that cabin you blowed up."

"Very likely," Slade agreed. "Well, he's tracking a long trail now, and I trust it slopes downward. I'll light the lamp and get coffee going; guess we could all stand a little about now. Then we'll pack the carcasses out and place them in the stable. Do you know Miss Jefferson?"

"I've seen the lady in town," replied Uncle Eben. "She favors her Pa for looks. Guess she favors him in shootin', too."

Pat came forward and extended her hand. "It's a pleasure to know you, Uncle Eben," she said. "And a great honor. I'll take care of the coffee," she added, glancing with a shudder at the bodies. "Please get those horrible things out of here."

"They're a lot better this way than they were alive," Slade said.

With Uncle Eben's help, he carried the bodies outside. As he turned over the one Pat shot, he paused, staring, and whistled under his breath.

It was the man who had conversed at length with Berne Rader in Sullivan's place the night before.

In the stable, Slade gave the bodies a careful once-over, hoping to find something of significance, but uncovered nothing of value save a considerable sum of money which he handed to Uncle Eben.

"Never mind, keep it," he said when the colored man was reluctant to accept it. "It'll help pay for those scorches you got on your wrists. I've a notion you need it more than the county treasury does, and that's where it'll go if the sheriff gets his paws on it."

Later, Slade slipped down the leg of his boot the running iron with which Uncle Eben's wrists had been burned. He thought that very likely it had also been used to run the brands on the horses.

By the time the chore at the stable was finished, Pat had coffee boiling and bacon and eggs sizzling in a skillet. Soon they sat down to a much-needed meal.

"And now what?" she asked, after they had finished eating.

"And now we're heading back to your ranchhouse, pronto," Slade said. "It'll be long past dark when we get there, as it is, and your Dad will very likely be having a conniption duckfit."

"Chances are he'll just think you and I have decided to stay out together all night," Pat replied, with a giggle. "A pity to disillusion him. And Uncle Eben is going with us," she declared firmly. "It isn't safe for him to stay here. Don't worry about your house, Uncle Eben. If anything happens to it, my father will gladly build you a better one, and furnish it, too."

"That would be mighty fine of him, ma'am," the old man answered. "But then, Mistuh Jefferson was always good to colored folks and poor people."

"She's right," said Slade. "Some more of those hellions might come nosing around, looking for the three that didn't show up again. Quite a few of them still left, I gather."

"Yes, guess there was a dozen or so of them in the beginning," said Uncle Eben. "But you're thinnin' 'em out, brother, you're thinnin' 'em out!"

Uncle Eben made a bundle of a few personal belongings, got the rig on Susie, the mule, and they set out on the long trip to the Diamond ranchhouse. As Slade predicted, it was hours past dark when they arrived.

Jefferson did not appear particularly perturbed. "Knew you were in good hands," he told his daughter. "But what happened, and where did you get him?" With a glance at Uncle Eben.

The story came out with a rush from Pat's lips, and lost nothing in the telling. Jefferson whitened a little as it progressed.

"Guess you were right in what you said this afternoon," he told Slade. "Never can tell who'll get hurt."

Then he shook hands warmly with the old colored man.

Uncle Eben was turned over to Steve Rafferty and the hands, who at once proceeded to make much of him.

"And you'd better stay right here with us, old feller," said Rafferty. "We can use you, and it's better than holin' up in that lonesome Thicket."

"I'm plumb obliged, suh, but I like the Thicket," Uncle Eben replied. "Never had any trouble there before."

"Everybody to their taste, as the old lady said when she kissed the cow," said Rafferty. "Come along, we're going to have some music and cards over to the bunkhouse."

Jefferson bethought himself of the words of old Manuel, the cook: "When *El Halcon* comes, the good rejoice, the evil tremble . . . When he departs, like the kindly wind he leaves behind him peace, and happiness, and content." Those words suddenly had a poignant meaning for Dunlap Jefferson.

"But I'm afraid my little gal is letting herself in for a heartache," he mused. "His sort don't often settle down. They ride the Lone Wolf Trail to the end appointed — 'to the Master of the workmen with the tally of their work.' "

When Pat went upstairs to change, Jefferson turned to Slade. "How about the horses those three rode?" he said.

"All three bore Diamond brands, slick-iron run," Slade replied. "We took the rigs off and turned them loose."

"But how about the one in my stable?" Jefferson asked.

"Hang onto it," Slade advised. "May come in handy."

"But if somebody should spot that slick-ironed brand, what then?" the ranchowner worried.

"I can say that it was not run by anyone with whom you have any connections," Slade answered. "And," with a slight smile, "I think my word will carry sufficient weight with the right people."

"I don't doubt it," grunted Jefferson. "If you tell them it's done in red, white and blue and several other colors, they won't argue the point. You're the limit!"

Slade laughed heartily, and changed the subject.

A little later, Jefferson chuckled. "The first killing credited to the Jefferson family since my dad's day," he remarked.

"It couldn't have happened at a better time for me," Slade declared with emphasis. "She sure saved my bacon. Mighty good shooting, too, over my shoulder to plug that devil dead center. I told her to stay at the edge of the clearing, but she followed me to the cabin."

"She did right," said Jefferson. "I'm proud of her."

"You have every right to be," Slade said.

Pat came down, scrubbed and rosy, and wearing a dress that Slade thought enhanced her charms.

"I'm hungry again," she said plaintively. "Suppose I go out to the kitchen and rustle something for all of us?"

"She's always hungry," said her father. "She'll make some cowhand a fine wife; he won't ever have to wait around for his chuck. Be on the table all the time."

Pat glanced at Slade, blushed prettily, and did not refute the charge.

After a good night's rest in an excellent bed, and a hearty breakfast, Slade was in the saddle the following morning. Jefferson had announced his intention of riding to Beaumont with him and when his horse was brought around, Slade noticed that there was a rifle in the saddle boot. Jefferson intercepted his glance.

"I'm taking no chances any more, not after what's been happening hereabouts," he said. "I only hope I get the chance to line sights with the hellion who did for poor Cliff Tevis, who was my range boss for years."

An expression of malignant hatred shadowed his comely features as he spoke, and Slade was convinced he meant it.

Pat came out and stood at the ranger's stirrup. "Come again, soon," she begged softly.

"I will," Slade promised, and meant it. He thought her even more charming than the night before, which, he thought with a chuckle, was something to reflect upon.

On arriving at Beaumont, they at once repaired to the sheriff's office, finding the old peace officer in. He listened with exasperated interest to Slade's story of the happenings of the day before.

"Three more, eh?" he snorted. "It's easy to track you by just following the trail of bodies."

"He only got two this time; Pat accounted for one," Jefferson put in proudly.

"Uh-huh, that's something else about him," said the sheriff. "He not only cashes people in right and left, but he starts folks who never shot at anything bigger than a coyote before to doing the same thing. Yes, I know Eben Prescott — been around here for the past two hundred years or so, and is all right. I'll pick him up at the ranchhouse and he can guide me to where the carcasses are laid away. I'll take a couple of deputies with me."

"Might be a good thing to take half a dozen," suggested Jefferson. "You might run into something up there."

"You could be right," agreed the sheriff. " 'Pears nobody is safe hereabouts any more. You going along, Jeff?"

"No, I have business in town," Jefferson said. He did not elaborate on just what that business was, but Slade heard about it that evening in the Crosby House lobby when Jim Hogg entered and plumped into a chair beside him.

"What's happened to your *amigo,* Dunlap Jefferson?" Hogg asked. "Has he gone loco or something?"

"Didn't show any signs of it yesterday or this morning," Slade replied. "Why?"

"Well, for some reason or other he sure appears to have experienced a change of heart," Hogg said. "Come up to me here this afternoon with a pleasant greeting.

Asked how I was making out with my ventures, and appeared really interested. A little later I heard that he had contacted Sid Wainright, who handles supplies for the field, and made a deal with him to run in a big herd of cows to provide badly needed meat. Heard, too, that he hunted up those fellers who wanted to drill on the open rangeland over to the west and told them to go ahead and drill till they hit China, for all he cared. Assured them there would be no interference. I can't understand it. Wouldn't be surprised if he sets up a rig on his own holdings next, the way he's done an about-face."

"That might be a notion," Slade said thoughtfully. Hogg shot him a keen glance.

"What do you mean, Slade?" he asked. "I know you're a darn good engineer and not given to making idle statements. What do you mean?"

"What I am going to say is largely conjecture on my part, although there are certain geological and petrological indications on which to base it," Slade replied slowly. "I consider it not unlikely that under Jefferson's land to the west of the field, at a much greater depth, is a second oil pool even larger than Spindletop. I think, sir, it would be a good idea for you to cultivate Dunlap

Jefferson. You might both profit greatly from the business."

Future developments, which are history, would prove Slade right in his surmise.

"You may have something there," Hogg agreed, his eyes showing definite interest. "Yes, I think I'll try and get on the right side of Jefferson. You really think such a pool might exist?"

"I think it is probable," Slade said. "And," he added reflectively, "it may provide an explanation for some of the things that have been happening in this section of late. I'm not the only engineer who isn't working at his profession, for one reason or another."

"You figure somebody may have the same notion?" asked Hogg.

"Not beyond the realm of possibility," Slade conceded. "It is something that would appeal to anybody with a strong gambling instinct."

"Right down Bet-a-Million Gates' alley," chuckled Hogg. "Did you ever hear the real story of how Gates got his nickname? The yarns about it are legion, but I know how it really happened. It goes back to the days when Gates was selling barbed wire to cowmen all over Texas, after convincing them that the wire would hold cattle in pasture.

"Gates and his partner, Ike Ellwood, the

barbed-wire manufacturer, were riding a train from Chicago to Pittsburgh. It was raining to beat the devil and a dreary day generally. Guess they'd got sort of bored with each other's company and didn't know what to do to break the monotony. Gates was looking out the window and started counting the raindrops gathering on the windowpane, and trickling down to the sill. All of a sudden he got an idea. 'Ellwood,' he said, 'tell you what we'll do to liven things up. I'll pick a drop and you pick a drop and I'll bet a million mine gets down first.'

" 'You're on,' said Ellwood, 'only we'll make it a thousand instead of a million. Let's go!'

"So away they went, betting on the drops running down the windowpane," chuckled Hogg. "Before they got to Pittsburgh, Gates had won twenty-two thousand dollars!"

Slade laughed heartily at the yarn. "Sounds like him, all right," he said. "Well, I've a notion he'll have the chance to do some heavy gambling in this section before all is said and done."

Hogg nodded. "Yes, that's Gates," he said. "He's never happy unless he's into something chancey up to his neck. He cares nothing for money as money, and very little for the things money will buy. Lives frugally as a sparrow on a twig, not from parsimony but because he just likes to live that way. For him the game is everything, win, lose, or draw."

The ex-governor paused, regarding his companion reflectively. "I think you and Gates have a good deal in common," he said slowly. "Yes, you're much the same type, only instead of investments, you gamble with lives, including your own."

Slade smiled, and did not comment.

"Speak about the devil!" Hogg exclaimed. "Here comes Gates now, picking his teeth. Guess he just finished eating."

The magnate waved Slade an airy greeting as he approached, but did not sit down; as usual, he was restless.

"What say, let's go over to Sullivan's and watch the game for a while," he suggested. "I was there before I ate. Berne Rader is sitting in and he 'pears to be in a mighty bad temper for some reason or other, although he appeared to be winning."

"Guess we could do worse," agreed Hogg.

When they reached the saloon, the game was going strong. Four oil men and Rader made up the table. As they stood watching the play, Bet-a-Million Gates suddenly had an inspiration.

"Slade," he said, "there's a vacant chair. Why don't you sit in a while?"

Slade shook his head. "Too steep for me," he declined.

"Don't let that bother you," urged Gates. "I'll back you. Please do it as a favor for me, won't you? I want to see if you're as good at poker as you are at everything else. Please!"

Slade hesitated, but an idea was building up in his mind. "All right," he said.

Gates slipped a packet of big bills into his hand. "If that don't hold you, there's plenty more where it came from," he whispered, and drew nearer the table.

"Gentlemen, my friend, Mr. Slade, would like to look at a hand or two," he said to the players. "Any objections?"

"Any friend of yours is welcome to join us, Mr. Gates," one of the oil men replied heartily. "Take a load off your feet, Mr. Slade, I'm just going to deal."

As he sat down opposite Berne Rader, Slade drew something from his boot top and laid it on the table. It was a recently scorched running iron.

"My lucky piece," he explained, with a smile.

The oil men laughed. Berne Rader stared at the slender steel rod with dilated eyes.

He wet his lips with the tip of his tongue, glanced at Slade, glanced back to the iron. Slade, whose eyes had never left the speculator's agitated face, smiled thinly, and peeped at his hole card.

As the game progressed, Rader played his cards badly. He couldn't seem to keep his eyes off Slade's "lucky piece" and did things that caused the other players to stare.

The game continued till well past midnight. By then, Slade was ahead a rather large sum. Then one of the oil men glanced at his watch.

"Guess that'll be all," he said. "Us fellers have to be on the job early; can't let pleasure interfere with business."

The game broke up. Berne Rader, without a glance at Slade, strode to the bar and ordered a drink which he downed at a gulp, following it with another for a chaser. Staring straight ahead, he left the saloon.

Slade made a neat packet of the money before him and handed it to Gates.

"Not a bad evening for you, sir," he said. "Guess you'll consider it chicken feed, but not bad."

"Hold on!" protested the magnate. "The winnings belong to you. You earned 'em."

Slade smilingly shook his head. "I have my winnings, big ones," he replied cryptically. "Let's go have a drink before bed."

As the ranger led the way to the bar, Gates muttered to Hogg, "Now just what the devil did he mean by that?"

"I don't know," Hogg confessed, "but I'll wager double against what you've got in your hand that somebody will find out, and won't like it."

In his room, Slade drew the "lucky piece" from his boot and turned it over and over in his slim fingers.

"You're not very hefty," he told the iron, "but I think you're hefty enough to trip a gallows trap. Now I really know just whom I'm after. All that remains is to drop a loop on the hellion; but that is likely to be something of a chore."

Sixteen

Before going down to breakfast the following morning, Slade sat for some time by the open window, smoking and thinking. At the moment the problem confronting him appeared almost insoluble. It was all very well to be convinced in his own mind that Berne Rader was the leader of the sinister band known as the Twilight Riders, but proving it and pinning his crimes onto that slippery customer was something else. His followers might be the ordinary type of bushpopping outlaws, but Rader was of more formidable calibre. A man well thought of by his associates, who apparently enjoyed considerable success in business matters and was undoubtedly far above the average in intelligence.

Slade conned over the recent events, beginning with the murder of Cliff Tevis, Dunlap Jefferson's range boss. He was of the opinion that Tevis had stumbled onto something, perhaps the fake brands and their author, and in so doing had sealed his own death warrant. He had possibly contacted the Twilight Riders and presumably accused them of slick-ironing the Diamond brand. Seeing that he was in for trouble, he had tried to escape, apparently heading for the shelter of the Big Thicket and was shot down before he could reach that dubious sanctuary.

The attempt to drygulch himself and Sheriff Colton came in for consideration. Undoubtedly the plot had been hatched in Beaumont, with the drygulcher circling around and reaching the Thicket before his intended victims. A smart attempt that very nearly succeeded.

The prints of high-heel boots at the scene of the dynamite explosion which wrecked the derrick and paved the way for the setting afire of the oil well had been a bit confusing at the time, leaning as it did to the notion that the Diamond outfit, tentatively under suspicion, might have been responsible.

But it was obvious that Rader's men, the majority of them at least, were or had been cowhands, and cowhands know how to handle dynamite. The oil-soaked dust in the overall pockets of the dead drygulcher indicated that he evidently had a man or two planted at the field to keep him posted on what went on there, but the drygulcher had worn rangeland garb.

And Slade had early discarded Dunlap Jefferson as a suspect. He just didn't fit into the picture properly; his methods were direct, witness his driving off the drillers from state land. His enmity for the oil people had been outspoken, coupled with threats against them. Nothing subtle about the procedure. Stupidly so, circumstances and conditions being what they were.

The derringer in Rader's sleeve was the first thing that started the ranger thinking about Rader, although in a vague way. It seemed strange that a man in Rader's supposed position would be packing a gun that way and very expertly executing the difficult "gambler's draw."

Rader's being on the railroad board of directors enabled him to obtain information not available to the general public, witness the supposedly secret payroll shipment on the train, which the Twilight Riders glommed onto.

He reflected on Rader's outburst during the poker game, when he, Slade, had prevented him from killing the oil man. He believed that right there was evidence of a weak spot in Rader's armor of respectability that might well prove his undoing — an ungovernable temper. Temper, which often blights a promising career of one sort or another, for a man who cannot control himself can seldom control others. Usually his control is a control based on fear, and fear begets hate and a thirst for vengeance. And there was another angle to consider.

The remarks of the bearded man, the companion of Dirk, the outlaw who got blown to the stars by the box of dynamite, had intimated that the boss of the Twilight Riders, Rader, also had a streak of sadistic cruelty in his makeup, which it appeared he practiced on his followers when they gave offence. Another weakness.

All in all, though he had practically nothing concrete to go on at the moment, Slade was fairly sanguine as to the ultimate outcome and believed that sooner or later he would be able to drop a loop on the callous and crafty speculator who, to judge from what the bearded man said, was playing for big stakes. Stakes that might well be tremendous, but were dependent on his tieing onto a portion, at least, of Dunlap Jefferson's holdings.

He glanced at the "lucky piece" running iron lying on the table. That, of course, had been the clincher. Rader's perturbation on seeing it in his possession had removed all doubt from the ranger's mind as far as Berne Rader was concerned. Right now, no doubt, Rader was wondering just how much that infernal *El Halcon* knew, and to what use he intended to put his knowledge.

Yes, he believed he could put Rader's number up.

Slade went down to breakfast in a fairly equable frame of mind. He had a problem on his hands that promised to tax even his ingenuity, and he had a disquieting premonition that he had never before had such an opponent as Berne Rader; but he felt that he had made some progress. At least, as Uncle Eben said, he was thinnin' 'em out, with a little help from Pat Jefferson. She was quite a gift, all right. Smart, charming, pretty as a spotted pony, with plenty of nerve and right there with a helping hand when it was needed most. Yes, she was hard to beat. He did not recall any woman he had met who intrigued him more, and he had met a few in his time. He resolved to ride to the Diamond ranchhouse at the earliest opportunity.

A pity the hellion she plugged didn't live long enough to talk a little! Very likely he had been Rader's right-hand man, and assigned the chore of luring *El Halcon* to Uncle Eben's cabin. Slade deduced that the news he brought Rader the night before in Sullivan's place, which so perturbed him, was that *El Halcon* had not been killed in the dynamite explosion which destroyed the hangout, but was still alive and kicking. Slade chuckled at thought of Rader's exasperation when he learned that his carefully laid plan had miscarried.

Slade spent an uneventful day loafing around Beaumont. Shortly after nightfall, he was sitting in the lobby of the Crosby House, when Sheriff Colton's chief deputy entered and approached him.

"The Old Man would like to see you in his office," the deputy announced.

Slade found Sheriff Colton seated at his desk, a perplexed look on his face. He motioned the ranger to a chair and for a moment regarded him in silence while filling and lighting his pipe.

"Sure one of those jiggers you plugged up at the thicket wasn't playing 'possum'?" he asked.

"I hardly think so," Slade replied. "Why?"

"Because when Eben Prescott and me and the boys got to the cabin there were only two carcasses waiting for us," the sheriff said. "Only two. We brought them to town. Quite a few folks have looked 'em over, but nobody recalls ever seeing them before. Everybody agrees one is an Injun."

Slade thoughtfully rolled a cigarette, gazing at the sheriff over the tobacco and paper. He lighted the brain tablet and asked, "Where are the bodies?"

"At the coroner's office, other side of the building," the sheriff answered.

"I'd like to take a look at them," Slade said.

Sheriff Colton stood up, turned the lamp down. "Let's go," he said, and led the way to the coroner's office. "There they are," he said, and was silent.

Slade gazed at the contorted faces. Yes, the Kiowa Indian was one of them. The other was broad and squat, with glazed muddy eyes and nondescript features. But missing was the man Pat Jefferson shot, the man who talked with Berne Rader in Sullivan's place and bent a gun barrel over the head of the belligerent rigger.

"Well?" said the sheriff.

"Well, it appears somebody didn't want the gent in question put on exhibition here in town," Slade said.

"You mean somebody here might have

seen him before?"

"Yes, several somebodies," Slade answered. "I know I did."

"The devil you say!"

"Yes, he was in Sullivan's place the other night. Had a row with an oil worker and belted him over the head with his gun barrel and knocked him out. Appeared to be a quiet sort, and a hard man."

"Well, I'll be hanged!" sputtered the sheriff.

"Not beyond the realm of possibility, perhaps," Slade conceded.

The sheriff swore. "So some of the hellions hang out right here in town, eh?" he growled. "Well, I figured as much. Why the devil did I ever stop following a cow's tail!"

"I've asked myself the same thing, once or twice," Slade admitted.

Sheriff Colton glowered at the two bodies, tugged his mustache, and glanced interrogatively at Slade.

"Let's go over to Sullivan's and have a talk with him and the bartenders," Slade suggested. "They'll recall the ruckus in there the other night and may remember something relative to that man. You ask the questions."

"That's a notion," said the sheriff. "Let's go!"

Sullivan readily recalled the incident and the man involved. "Been in here quite a few times," he replied to the sheriff's question. "Cowhand, all right, but I don't remember him ever saying who he worked for. Always had money. Quiet sort, but seemed ready enough to talk with anybody who happened to speak to him, as folks will at a bar. First time he ever had any trouble here, and it wasn't his fault the other night. Sure took care of it fast and proper. Reckon that big oil worker never knew what hit him. He was talking to himself when we shoved him out the back door and sent him on his way."

"Well, we didn't learn much," observed the sheriff, after Sullivan left them.

"No, except that the fellow hung around town," Slade agreed. "Which eventually may prove important," he added thoughtfully.

"Guess he wasn't the only one of the hellions prowlin' around here," growled the sheriff.

"No, certainly not the only one," Slade nodded.

Slade spent two more quiet days in Beaumont. Berne Rader was conspicuous by his absence. Gates and Jim Hogg speculated on his whereabouts and what deal he might be concocting.

"I'll bet a million he and the Kountz interests are cooking up something, very likely something we won't like," complained the former. "That hellion is a smooth article. Wish I knew what the devil he's up to."

Slade wished the same, for different reasons. Gradually he experienced uneasiness. He wondered if Rader, having gotten a good scare, had pulled out for good, although he thought that unlikely. The third morning, still pondering the problem, he saddled up and headed for the Diamond ranchhouse. Perhaps he'd learn something there. At least he'd see Pat Jefferson, which was not an unpleasant prospect. He rode slowly, keeping a watch on his surroundings and at the same time endeavoring to put himself in Rader's place and considering what he would do under similar circumstances, a habit with *El Halcon,* his long experience with the workings of the outlaw mind having developed a certain familiarity with its tortuous processes.

Rader was playing for big stakes. Would he abandon the project because, in his opinion, another shrewd and daring owlhoot was endeavoring to horn in on the game? Slade was fairly confident that Rader had no idea that he, Slade, was a Texas Ranger. Believing that he only had an individual to deal with, wouldn't Rader be more likely to resolve to pit his wits against *El Halcon's*? Especially as he had an organization at his back while thinking *El Halcon* played a lone hand. After carefully considering every angle, Slade arrived at the conclusion that Rader wouldn't pull out. But, in the words of Bet-a-Million Gates, what the devil was he cooking up?

While there was strength in having an outfit, there was also a weakness. Such a bunch had to be supplied with money, and there was little doubt, Slade believed, that Rader had to pull jobs to get the needed wherewithal to keep his band together and working with him. Very likely, he thought, right now Rader was planning some raid that would net him a fat profit, with murder, if necessary, or even wantonly, an accessory. Which gave the ranger much concern. Already too many innocent people had died because of Rader's depredations.

When Slade drew rein at the veranda of the Diamond casa, Pat came dancing down the steps to greet him.

"So you did decide to come back!" she exclaimed.

"How could I keep from it?" he asked as he dismounted.

"Sounds nice, and I like to hear it, but I fear that, like Steve Rafferty, you are addicted to flattery."

"When was flattery lost on woman's ear?" Slade misquoted.

"Oh, I guess we all love it, even though we don't believe it," she replied gaily. "Anyhow, I'm glad to see you. Come on in; here comes Bob Gilman to look after Shadow; he fell in love with that horse when you were here before. Says he's the sort worth getting hanged for to steal; you unscramble it."

"Guess I gather the general meaning," Slade smiled. "Hello, Bob. Shadow remembers you."

The wrangler proudly led the great black to the stable. Slade and Pat entered the living room.

"How's Uncle Eben?" he asked.

Pat was instantly serious. "I'm worried about him," she replied. "He insisted on riding to the Thicket early this morning. Said he had some business to attend to there, but that he would be back tonight or early tomorrow. Said he hoped you'd show up here soon, that he might have something to tell you."

Slade's brows drew together. "Hope he didn't return to his cabin," he said. "Some of those devils might be hanging around there expecting him to do just that. They're a vicious lot. If he doesn't show up in the morning, I'll go looking for him."

"And I'll go with you," Pat said.

"You will not," he told her flatly. "One experience like you had there is enough."

"Came in rather handy, didn't I?"

"You certainly did," he conceded, "but I don't care to subject you to such a risk again."

Pat said nothing more, but there was a set to her chin that made him uneasy.

It was a tired old man who rode in to the ranchhouse long after dark. Pat at once haled him into the kitchen, where it was warm and comfortable, and set before him a bountiful meal prepared by her own hands. When she was out of the room for a few minutes, Uncle Eben turned to Slade.

"I found it, brother," he said.

"Yes?" Slade prompted.

"Yes, I found the Twilight Riders' new hangout. Somehow had a notion where they might go and went to see. Not many folks know the Thicket like I do, but 'pears one of those scalawags knows it mighty well, too. An old, old cabin smack on the bank of Lost

Bayou. Wouldn't be surprised if the Injun feller you killed showed 'em to it. Hardly anybody nowadays knows about that cabin, but way, way back, oldtimers knew about it and said it was built and lived in by a mighty bad man who used to rob folks and feed 'em to the 'gators. Bayou's full of 'gators — whoppers. Mighty hard to come by, that cabin, but I know the trail. Not so over-far back the Thicket, but a awful wild spot, with thick woods all around it. Ghost woods, colored folks call 'em. Say ha'nts live there. Don't take much stock in ha'nts. It's the live ones you gotta watch out for. Dead folks don't hurt nobody."

"You're right there," Slade agreed. "And you feel pretty sure it's the Twilight Riders and not just some settler who hankers for peace and solitude?"

"Yes, I'm sure," replied Uncle Eben. "A lot of horses have used that old trail plumb recent, and I reckon there ain't been a horse on it before for years. When I got along toward where the cabin is, I hitched Susie in the brush and then snuck ahead on foot until I got to where I could see the cabin. There was smoke coming out of the chimney. I holed up in the brush and watched. After a while a feller came out for water from a spring. A big, broad feller with lots of black whiskers."

Slade nodded. The description pretty well fitted Dirk's bearded companion the night he was kidnapped and taken to the outlaw hangout.

"I stayed around quite a spell," Uncle Eben resumed, "until it was getting close to dark, and mighty gloomy already in the Ghost Woods. Figured I'd better be getting out of there. Didn't want to meet some more of those varmints on the trail. Slipped back and got Susie and headed for home. So what we going to do about it, brother?"

"Frankly, I don't know," Slade admitted. "No law, so far as I know of, against people consorting in a cabin in the Thicket. About the only charge that could be placed against them would be a mighty shaky one of unlawful assembly. Doubtful if even that would stand up in court, and would mean little if it did. Necessary to get some real proof of wrong-doing before cracking down on them."

"Going to tell the sheriff about it?" asked Uncle Eben.

"Perhaps, haven't decided yet," Slade answered.

"Guess you got all the law authority you need, without the sheriff," Uncle Eben observed significantly, with a keen glance at his table companion. "I got my notions about you, brother."

"Yes, I think I have," Slade admitted with a smile. "The problem is, how to use it."

"There'll come a way," Uncle Eben predicted confidently.

"Yes, but meanwhile some more innocent people may die," Slade replied gloomily. For some moments he sat in silence. Then,

"If you feel up to it, tomorrow you and I will take a little ride through your Ghost Woods," he said. "I'd like to get to that cabin about dark and watch through the night. Okay with you?"

"Okay with me, brother," said Uncle Eben.

Pat returned at that moment and the conversation ceased.

"All finished?" she asked. "Now you smoke a pipe, Uncle Eben, and then to bed with you. You don't want to overdo it."

"That's right, ma'am," the colored man agreed. "Old bones need their rest."

"Old!" scoffed Pat. "You're spry as a gopher. I only hope I'm as chipper as you when I'm your age."

"Don't worry, ma'am, you will be," Uncle Eben replied. "You and Mistuh Slade both. I can hear you both right now, when you're seventy, telling your younkers, 'This up-

and-comin' gen'ration ain't got the stuff we had when we were young.' "

Slade laughed. Pat blushed rosily. "I hope so," she said, with a little sigh.

SEVENTEEN

Shortly before noon the following day, Slade and Uncle Eben rode for the Big Thicket. Slade noticed that the colored man had a saddle boot attached to his rig. He stared when Uncle Eben drew forth what it contained.

"Holy smoke! a double-barreled six-gauge shotgun!" he exclaimed. "I think that's only the second one I ever saw. If you cut loose with that old baseburner, you'll blow the whole Thicket clean to Louisiana!"

"She usually gets what she goes after," Uncle Eben said complacently, patting the weapon before restoring it to its scabbard.

"I should think she would, and everything else in the immediate vicinity," Slade agreed. "Where'd you get her?"

"Had her in the cabin, got her years ago," said Uncle Eben. "Yesterday I made certain there weren't none of those scalawags around and slipped in and got her and toted her along with me. Figured she might come in handy. They won't catch me settin' again. I'd oughta knowed when they rode up to the cabin that they weren't up to no good. I moved a mite too slow and they grabbed me. Won't happen again."

They reached the Thicket somewhat to the north of where the trail from Uncle Eben's cabin led to the prairie. The old man did not hesitate but entered the growth at a certain point. They continued steadily for several miles along a faint and grass-grown track. Uncle Eben turned sharply to the right, turned again to the left, and announced,

"We're goin' into the Ghost Woods now. Here's the track."

Slade quickly noted that the trail, while largely overgrown with grass and shrubs, was sunk nearly a foot into the soil and was fairly broad. It was evidently very old and doubtless had been beaten out by myriad moccasined feet when the Indians roved the section, long before the white man came. And, like Uncle Eben the day before, he saw that a number of horses had passed that way only a short time previous, and that there were no old prints visible. Looked like the old man was right; he had really found the new hangout of the Twilight Riders.

Also, he quickly decided that the Ghost Woods were aptly named. The height of the trees and the thickness of the boles were tremendous, shooting upward in magnificent columns until, far above, they threw out their side branches in Gothic upward curves which coalesced to form one great matted roof of verdure, through which only an occasional golden ray of sunshine shot downward to trace a thin dazzling line of light amidst the majestic obscurity.

To add to the weirdness of the scene, both trunks and boughs were clothed with a long gray species of ochella moss, which even in the early afternoon gave the place a ghostly appearance. Slade thought he had seldom seen anything more remarkable than the appearance of one of those mighty trees festooned from top to bottom with trailing wreaths of the sad-hued moss, in which the wind whispered gently as it stirred them. At a distance it looked like the gray locks of a Titan crowned with green leaves and here and there starred with the rich bloom of orchids.

Yes, the Ghost Woods lived up to their name, and had Slade believed in "ha'nts," as Uncle Eben called them, he would have been inclined to think that this was indeed their home. However, the fresh prints in the soft earth of the old trail more than hinted that here would very likely be found things much more deadly than haunts or other fabled denizens of the unseen world. Only the whispering of the wind, the soft pad of the hoofs of horse and mule and an occasional bird call broke the cathedral hush.

Mile after mile they rode. The shadows lengthened, the gray twilight purpled, birds called their sleepy notes. Uncle Eben slowed the pace and began studying the growth to the right.

"Here's where we turn off and leave the critters," he said. "Little grass spot over there by a crick."

They pushed through the tangle until they reached the bank of a small stream. Here they dismounted, loosened the cinches and turned their mounts loose to graze. Then, returning to the trail, they stole forward on foot, covering something like half a mile before Uncle Eben veered again, holding up his hand for silence; a dozen yards or so through thick growth and he turned to move parallel to the trail. A few more minutes and they squatted at the fringe of the brush and peered forth.

The Ghost Woods had been weird enough, but the scene upon which Slade gazed was even more so. They were at the edge of a fairly wide, almost circular clearing, which, fringed on three sides by the jungle tangle, was like an inverted funnel. The fourth side opened onto a black and melancholy body of water, its glassy surface reflecting the red, sunset sky. No ripple stirred it. There was no lapping against the clay bank. Dark, mysterious, perfectly smooth, it stretched on and on into the distance.

"Lost Bayou," Uncle Eben whispered. "The Injuns say that once upon a time, long ago, a big village was there. Said the Great Spirit one day told the chief to get outa there and head for higher ground. Chief didn't pay him no mind and when him and a bunch of his braves got back from hunting they found the water had come up from the ground and covered the whole place. The Injuns called the section the 'tremblin' ground' and said the earthquake the Great Spirit told the chief was coming made the Bayou. Could have been, I reckon."

Slade nodded without speaking, his attention fixed on something else. Standing on the very bank of the bayou was an old cabin, much worn by wind and weather, but apparently tight enough. Very silently it stood. No smoke rose from its mud-and-stick chimney. No gleam of light showed behind its dirty windowpanes. A nearby lean-to was empty.

"Looks like there's nobody home," he breathed.

"Looks that way," agreed Uncle Eben. "Better wait a while, though; might be fellers in there, sleepin'."

Slade nodded and they settled down in the growth to watch and wait. Finally he became convinced that the building was tenantless.

"I'm going to try and get a peek through one of those windows before it gets too dark to see inside," he told his companion. "Cover the door with your cannon, but don't pull trigger unless you figure you have to." Before Uncle Eben could protest, he slid out of the concealing growth.

Crossing the clearing was a ticklish business; at any moment explosive life might erupt back of those shadowy panes. He breathed a sigh of relief when he reached the cabin wall. Edging along it, he peered through a window.

It was already very gloomy inside, but he could make out bunks built against the walls and covered with blankets, a table and chairs, cooking utensils beside the wide fireplace. There was little doubt that the shack had known recent occupancy. He started to enter, but decided against it; he might leave some trace of his presence which would warn the outlaws that something was amiss. He returned to where Uncle Eben waited, shotgun trained on the door.

"We'll stick around a while and see if anybody shows up," he said. "Reckon we can risk a smoke."

They lighted a pipe and cigarette and settled down comfortably in the growth. The darkness deepened. High in the west a great star glowed and trembled. In the east a huge orange moon rose, a fit lamp for the eerie setting below.

Suddenly the night was filled with plaintive and heart-rending cries, cries as of children in distress, like the wail of all the babies since the world began. They ceased abruptly, then started again with redoubled intensity.

Uncle Eben chuckled. "Know what that is, brother?" he asked.

"Yes," Slade replied. "I've heard it before. It's the alligators singing. The bayou must be full of them."

"Big ones, too," said Uncle Eben. "Real whoppers. Yep, that's the 'gators, but a lot of folks'll tell you it ain't true. They'll tell you it's babies cryin' for their murdered

241

fathers that were throwed in the bayou for the 'gators to eat."

"Small blame to them," said Slade. "It's one devil of a racket."

" 'Gators are hungry," Uncle Eben remarked meditatively. "Always bawl like that when the moon's up and they're hungry. Don't want to go foolin' too close to the water. Out comes a tail and smacks you plumb into the bayou and down into a 'gator's belly."

For minutes the uncanny cacophony continued, then ceased as suddenly as it began.

Four tedious hours passed, and the better part of a fifth. The great clock in the sky was wheeling westward, the moon had passed the zenith. Slade was thinking seriously of giving up the wearisome vigil when Uncle Eben uttered a warning hiss and held up his hand for silence.

"Horses coming on the trail," he whispered.

Straining his ears, Slade also could hear the muffled hoofbeats that steadily loudened. They passed where the pair crouched motionless, and a moment later, shapes loomed in the clearing. Slade counted six horsemen. The one slightly in the lead was tall and broad-shouldered, but his face, turned slightly sideways, was but a whitish blur in the uncertain moonlight.

The group rode to the lean-to and dismounted. There was a thumping and rustling in the gloom under the lean-to, as of corn or grain dumped into mangers. Then the six reappeared on foot, walked to the cabin door and entered, closing the door behind them.

"Some of those fellers were totin' saddle pouches with them," breathed Uncle Eben. "Looks like they got something; something that belongs to other folks, the chances are."

"Very likely," Slade agreed.

The window panes became rectangles of gold as lamps were lighted inside the cabin. A few minutes later smoke spiraled up from the chimney.

"Going to rustle some chuck," muttered Uncle Eben. "Looks like they're here to stay a while. What we going to do, brother? Six of the devils."

"Nothing, yet," Slade replied. "We'll watch a while and see what happens. Still nothing we can jump them for, as far as I can see."

They settled down in their leafy burrow again, eyes fixed on the cabin, from which came the sound of voices and a banging and rattling of pans. Slade earnestly desired to get another look through the window and debated with himself the advisability of such a course. He'd wait a while. Perhaps the bunch would get sleepy and make the undertaking less risky. Something like an hour dragged by.

Suddenly from within the cabin came the sound of voices raised in loud altercation. There was a volley of oaths and a cry of pain.

"Now, what in blazes?" Slade wondered.

"Sounds like they're having a bobberty among themselves," said Uncle Eben. "Maybe they'll start shooting," he added hopefully.

The uproar in the cabin loudened. There was the crash of an overturned chair, a despairing howl. The door banged open and through it bulged a tangle of figures, in their midst a man who yelled and struggled.

Straight to the bayou bank they rushed him. A heave of brawny arms and, screeching, he arced out over the water to land with a resounding splash.

Instantly the surface of the bayou seethed and boiled. A scream of agony and terror knifed the air, crescendoed to a frightful, bubbling shriek, and chopped off short. There followed a churning of the water to suds, the crunching of great jaws, and shouts of raucous laughter from the five men on the bank. Chuckling loudly, they turned and trooped back into the cabin.

EIGHTEEN

Walt Slade sank back in the growth, the palms of his hands moist, sweat beading his temples. Then he straightened to his full height. His face was set like granite, his eyes the color of frosted steel.

"That's all we need," he said. "It was murder, and we both witnessed it. Are you game to follow me to that cabin, Uncle Eben?"

"Yes, brother, I'll follow you — I'll be right 'longside of you," the old man answered. "I sorta want a chance to even up for these scorches on my wrists."

"Okay," Slade said. He drew something from a secret pocket in his broad leather belt and pinned it to his shirtfront. It was the famous silver star set on a silver circle, the feared and honored badge of the Texas Rangers.

Uncle Eben didn't appear particularly surprised. "Been rather thinking so for quite a spell," he said. "We all set to go?"

"Hold up your right hand," Slade replied. "I'll deputize you, so if something happens to me you'll be in the clear. We'll cross the clearing at a run and I'll hit the door with my shoulder and knock it open. We should be on top of them before they realize what's up. They don't deserve it, but I'm a law enforcement officer and I have to give them a chance to surrender. If they resist, shoot fast and shoot straight. If they get the best of us, *we'll* feed the alligators."

"Old Betsy here had oughta take care of about half of 'em when she opens up," Uncle Eben replied cheerfully, cocking both barrels of the huge weapon. "I'm all ready."

"Wait," Slade said. "First, I wish to make sure the man I most want is in there. I'm pretty sure he is, but I'm going to chance another look through the window."

"Slide around in the shadow to the bayou bank and sneak up to the cabin that way," advised Uncle Eben. "Don't get too close to the water; the 'gators are watching and waiting."

Slade nodded and sped around the circle of the clearing with swift, light steps. He reached the cabin without arousing alarm and edged along the wall until he could see through the window.

The five men were sitting around the table, on which was a pile of money — rolls of gold coin, packets of bills, which one man was counting.

Slade experienced a grim satisfaction. The money counter was Berne Rader. Turning, he glided back to where Uncle Eben waited.

"He's there," he told the colored man. "All set? Let me keep a little in front, so we won't jostle each other when I hit the door. Let's go!"

They raced across the clearing, Slade a step ahead. He hit the door with his shoulder, all his two hundred pounds of bone and muscle behind it. The door slammed open and they were in the room. Slade's voice rolled forth.

"In the name of the State of Texas, I arrest Berne Rader and others for robbery and murder! Anything you say —"

Berne Rader screamed, the cackling screech of a madman. His right hand shot forward. The double-barreled derringer slapped against his palm.

Slade fired point-blank. Rader yelled with pain as the heavy slug smashed the derringer from his hand, taking a finger with it. His companions were coming to their feet, reaching for their guns.

Uncle Eben's six-gauge let go, both barrels, with a crash that shook the building and filled the room with blinding smoke. With amazing speed he flipped the breech open and shoved in fresh cartridges. Slade was shooting with both hands, although all he could see to shoot at was shifting shadows.

A falling man knocked the table over. It caught Slade on the knees and flailed him off his feet. As he went down, he clutched to save himself and his guns clattered on the floor.

Over the wreckage leaped Berne Rader, going like the wind. Slade surged to his feet, dived forward and caught him just as he went out the door. Rader twisted about and they closed in a furious wrestle. Uncle Eben dared not take his eyes off the two men cowering under the muzzles of his shotgun, ready to take a chance if his vigilance relaxed for an instant.

Back and forth Slade and his opponent reeled, sliding and bumping along the cabin wall. Rader was a big man, not as tall but pounds heavier than the ranger, and he fought with maniacal fury. He got a throttling grip on Slade's throat and held on, heedless of the blows that crashed into his face.

Slade's head was swimming. His chest

heaved and labored as he fought for air. He tore at Rader's wrist with one hand, blocked blows with the other and countered blindly.

They crashed into the corner of the building, lurched back, now on the very edge of the black water a few feet below. Slade knew his strength was draining away. Red flashes stormed before his eyes. His heart fluttered like a caged bird. Rader, blood and foam on his lips, was mouthing curses, his eyes were like coals of fire. He forced the ranger back a step. The muscles of his arm swelled as he put forth a final effort. The strain on Slade's cervical vertebrae was almost beyond endurance. With the strength of despair he hurled himself backward and down, gripping Rader's wrist.

He struck on his back with stunning force. Rader catapulted over him. His grip was torn from *El Halcon's* throat, and Slade let go his wrist.

Through the air Rader shot, his body revolving. He cleared the bank and plunged into the bayou.

Again came that boiling and churning of the water; again an awful shriek of agony. There was a crunching and grinding of huge teeth, a strident bellowing, and silence.

Slade got slowly to his feet, breathing in great gasps. He cast a look of horror at the black water, now motionless. He could feel gleaming eyes regarding him hopefully. He shuddered, a crawling nausea in the pit of his stomach, and stumbled back to the cabin door.

Uncle Eben still stood with his shotgun trained on the two surviving outlaws.

"You all right, brother?" he asked anxiously, without turning his head.

"I'm okay, only I feel uncommonly like being sick," Slade replied. "Listening to alligators at table twice in one night is a little too much."

"They sure ain't got nice eating manners," said Uncle Eben.

With a nod of profound agreement, Slade picked up his fallen guns, ejected the spent shells and replaced them with fresh cartridges from his belts.

"All right," he told the owlhoots. "Face against the wall, hands behind you. Don't make any funny moves. I'm in the notion to watch somebody die a clean death for a change."

The outlaws did not appear to see anything humorous in the remark. They scowled, and obeyed. Uncle Eben lowered his shotgun with a relaxed sigh.

"There should be some tie ropes or something in the lean-to," Slade told him. "Get them and truss up these gents. Then we'll straighten out this mess a bit and have some coffee; I see there's a pot steaming on the coals."

The outlaws were quickly secured and seated in chairs against the wall. The overturned table was righted. The money had been scattered over the floor, but after a search, Slade and Uncle Eben recovered all of it, which they heaped on the table. Slade sat down facing the captives.

"Where'd you get it?" he asked, gesturing to the money. "Better talk. I can't promise anything, but if you come clean I will say a word for you that may make it easier for you when you come to trial." He paused expectantly.

"The Voth bank," one of the men replied sullenly. "We cleaned it yesterday."

"Kill anybody this time?"

The man shook his head. "Nope, didn't have to. We caught 'em settin', and we were masked."

"And why did you chuck that poor devil into the bayou a little while ago?"

"He was holding out some yellow boys. Boss said to get rid of him. He liked to feed the 'gators."

"And ended up feeding them with himself," grunted Uncle Eben. "He had it coming."

"What do you know about Rader?" Slade asked.

"Not much," the prisoner replied. "Ran into him over in New Mexico. He was dealing cards there and doing a little stealing on the side. He was an educated feller, and smart. Showed us how to get real money. Things were getting sort of hot and we moved over here. He knew the section — dealt cards on the Sabine boats once. Knew all about this blasted Thicket, too. Told us he had something big in mind. Wouldn't say what it was — wouldn't ever talk about anything if he didn't have to. Don't know what it was, 'cept he said it was big and would put us all on Easy Street. Somehow it depended on getting rid of that ranching feller, Dunlap Jefferson. We kept stirring up trouble with the oil people and making it look like Jefferson was responsible. He kept sounding off against the oil field all the time, which helped. Rader figured to kill those fellers drilling over west of Jefferson's holding and spread the story around that Jefferson did it, after telling them to go ahead and drill so he'd get a chance to drygulch them. Rader figured the oil workers would lynch Jefferson."

"Probably would have, or would have tried to," Slade conceded soberly. "Why did you kill Jefferson's range boss?"

"He caught onto our slick-ironin' the Diamond brand on our horses. Ran into us out on the range and braced us about it. We had to get rid of him. He knew Rader in town."

Slade nodded, and drank some coffee. "Well, guess that's about all," he said. "Be getting light shortly and we'll head for town." He crossed the room and gazed at the two bodies sprawled beside a bunk. One was the heavy-set, bearded man who accompanied Dirk the night of the kidnapping; the other, the individual who posed as a deputy sheriff.

"We'll tie them to a couple of horses and take them along with us," he told Uncle Eben. "Sheriff will want to see them."

"Mistuh Colton's going to be a mighty surprised man," chuckled Uncle Eben. "Reckon Mistuh Jefferson will be, too. Got a notion Miss Pat done figured you out pretty well all the time. Ain't easy to fool a woman, 'specially when she likes a man."

The sheriff was not as surprised as Uncle Eben anticipated. "Didn't know for sure just what brand you were wearing," he admitted, "but figured whatever it was it must be okay. That's why I strung along with you all the time and didn't put much stock in that *El Halcon* foolishness. Figured you knew your business and would open up when and if you were of a mind to."

Bet-a-Million Gates was surprised, and enthusiastic. "Right where you belong, right where you belong," he declared. "Nothing in the world like the Texas Rangers. Wish I had the guts and ability to be one myself. Real gambling! Real gambling! And Jim Hogg knew all along, eh? Can't ever get anything out of Hogg, he's so darned secretive. Rader had us all fooled, though. We knew he was a smooth article but didn't guess he was plumb off-color. Now what?"

"Now," said Slade, "Uncle Eben and I are going to get something to eat, and sleep the clock around. Then I'll be moving. Chances are Captain Jim will have something lined up for me by the time I get back to the post. I'll stop and see Jefferson on my way."

They didn't quite sleep the clock around, but didn't miss it too much. The following morning they headed for the Diamond spread.

"After what Manuel, the cook, told me, I'm not over-surprised, either," said Jefferson. "Manuel don't often make mistakes. But *El*

Halcon being a Texas Ranger sort of takes the hide off the barn door!"

"Yes, I'll come back," were Slade's last words to Pat. "A ranger rides a lone trail and a long trail, but there never was a trail that didn't have a turning, and sometimes it comes back to right where it started."

They watched him ride away, with a song on his lips and laughter in his eyes, to where duty called and new adventure waited.

"Manuel was right," observed Jefferson. "Behind him he leaves peace, and happiness, and content."

His daughter answered, "Not quite!"

We hope you have enjoyed this Large Print book. Other Thorndike, Wheeler, and Chivers Press Large Print books are available at your library or directly from the publishers.

For information about current and upcoming titles, please call or write, without obligation, to:

Publisher
Thorndike Press
295 Kennedy Memorial Drive
Waterville, ME 04901
Tel. (800) 223-1244

or visit our Web site at:

www.gale.com/thorndike
www.gale.com/wheeler

OR

Chivers Large Print
published by BBC Audiobooks Ltd
St James House, The Square
Lower Bristol Road
Bath BA2 3SB
England
Tel. +44(0) 800 136919
email: bbcaudiobooks@bbc.co.uk
www.bbcaudiobooks.co.uk

All our Large Print titles are designed for easy reading, and all our books are made to last.